THROUGH GOYA'S EYES:

THE WORLD OF THE SPANISH PAINTER AND HIS FRIEND AND MENTOR, GASPAR JOVELLANOS

by Dorothy Ricci

Royal Fireworks
Unionville, New York

DEDICATION:

To Matthew, Katie, Sara, and Amanda, with love.

Library of Congress Cataloging-in-Publication Data

Ricci, Dorothy.
  Through Goya's eyes : the world of the Spanish painter
and his friend and mentor, Gaspar Jovellanos / by Dorothy
Ricci.
        p. cm.
  Summary: In 1757 to 1811 Spain, as liberal patriot Gaspar
Jovellanos strives for reforms against ignorance, su-
perstition, and the Inquisition, he makes many powerful
enemies but finds comfort in good friends, including the
painter, Franscisco Goya.
  ISBN 978-0-88092-762-8 (library binding : alk. paper) --
ISBN 978-0-88092-763-5 (pbk. : alk. paper)
  1. Jovellanos, Gaspar de, 1744-1811--Fiction. 2. Goya,
Francisco, 1746-1828--Fiction. [1. Jovellanos, Gaspar de,
1744-1811--Fiction. 2. Reformers--Fiction. 3. Inquisition-
-Spain--Fiction. 4. Goya, Francisco, 1746-1828--Fiction.
5. Artists--Fiction. 6. Spain--History--18th century--
Fiction. 7. Spain--History--19th century--Fiction.] I.
Title.
  PZ7.R3552Thr 2008
  [Fic]--dc22
                                              2008012820

Royal Fireworks Press
First Avenue, PO Box 399
Unionville, NY 10988-0399
(845) 726-4444
FAX: (845) 726-3824
email: mail@rfwp.com
website: rfwp.com

ISBN: 978-0-88092-762-8 Library Binding
ISBN: 978-0-88092-763-5 Paperback

Printed and bound in the United States of America using vegetable-
based inks on acid-free, recycled paper and environmentally-friendly
cover coatings by the Royal Fireworks Printing Co. of Unionville,
New York.

CONTENTS

Castile 1797

Asturias 1798

Majorca 1801

Castile 1808

Asturias 1811

CHAPTER ONE
Gaspar and Goya

T he wind whipped Gaspar's dark blond hair as he dashed up the pebbly trail. Chasing him, his older brother Francisco de Paula slipped in the loose scree, lost his footing, and fell on one knee. In a flash the boys' friend, eight-year-old Juan Ceán Bermúdez, leaped over him and raced after Gaspar.

Reaching the crest of the hill, Gaspar collapsed on his back under the leafy boughs of a large oak tree, the grass warm and dry beneath him. His brother and Juan plopped down next to him, panting.

"I won," Gaspar chuckled, looking up through the branches toward the deep blue summer sky.

"I slipped," Francisco protested, grinning, "and I was gaining on you." He brushed aside the dried grass that his brother tossed at him.

Thirteen-year-old Gaspar Jovellanos lived in Asturias, the northern, green region of Spain. He sat up and looked out over the blue sparkle of the Cantabrian Sea.

"It's a splendid day," he observed, his dark eyes glancing down the coastline to where his city lay hugging the shore. "Bright and clear. Gijón at its finest."

It was Francisco's turn to toss a handful of grass. Gaspar brushed it off and gathered another clump to aim at his brother.

"I wish you didn't have to go," Juan interrupted wistfully.

Gaspar grinned and tossed the grass playfully at his young friend.

"Why can't your parents send one of your brothers instead," Juan persisted. "Why can't you go, Francisco? You're just a year older than Gaspar."

"Me?" Francisco asked, startled, eyes wide. "Send me to become a priest? I'm too wild for that!"

"That's the problem," Juan continued. "You're too good, Gaspar. You study too much, and you're too kind to everyone, too quiet, too well-behaved. That's why they chose you to go."

"He can be pretty wild," Francisco protested. "Have you ever seen him riding? He's always galloping his horse like a wild man." He laughed at his description.

"No...no," Juan responded. "You need to do something bad, Gaspar. Something to make your parents change their minds about sending you away to school. Then we could all still be together."

Gaspar turned his gaze from his city and looked at the young boy.

"Bermudo," he said kindly, using the child's nickname, "My parents have eight children. From their four sons, they have chosen me for a life in the Church. I am going away to school to study and to learn."

"Maybe if you didn't read so much," the child persisted, his thoughts expanding on ways to ruin his friend's reputation, "or if you didn't behave so well in church. There's still time, Gaspar, for you to do something really bad to change their minds."

"You're right, Bermudo," Francisco said soberly, "Gaspar is very intelligent. My parents must have known he would be. That is why they gave him such a long name, Gaspar Melchor Baltasar. They knew that he would be able to spell it when he was a little boy."

"I was born on the fifth of January," Gaspar explained, "and I was named for the Three Kings."

"And you're also right, Bermudo, about his excellent behavior," Francisco went on, grinning mischievously, "but he has managed to fool everyone. No one knows how bad he really is." He sighed, hands tucked under his head, gazing heavenward. "Only his patient, forgiving brother knows."

"Gaspar, will you think about it?" Juan pleaded. "We can still plan something."

Gaspar plucked some grass, but tossed it toward the water below them lapping quietly at the shore.

"I won't be going away forever, Bermudo. I'll be home for vacations and, besides, I'm only going to Oviedo and probably Avila afterwards. Actually, I'm pretty excited about it. I've never been south to the Meseta." He looked wistfully at the green trees shading the hill. "And I'll be back for holidays, and we'll still be friends."

"It won't be the same," Juan said quietly, "It will never be the same."

Southeast of Gijón, in the city of Zaragoza, province of Aragon, an eleven-year-old barefoot boy tucked a small cloak under his arm and raced along a walled enclosure. Reaching a wooden gate, he paused to push dark, rumpled hair from his forehead.

Peering into the enclosure, sharp, black eyes narrowing in the intense sunlight, a grin of satisfaction spread slowly across his plump, round face.

"Oo, *Toro*," he cooed softly. "Today you will face the great matador."

Slipping silently through the slats of the gate, he slowly unfurled the cloak.

"Eh, *Toro*," he called, standing rigidly upright, the cloak before him.

The young bull, grazing quietly, glanced up at the intruder but returned his attention to the grass.

"Eh, you, *Toro*," the boy shouted, stamping his foot to activate his opponent. The munching continued.

Suddenly, a harsh shout split the silence of the enclosure, startling the young bull and sending the boy dashing toward the gate. Diving through the slats, he fled down the path, angry words in his ears.

"Get out of here! I catch you again with my bulls, you will be very sorry. You hear me, Goya?"

At a safe distance, the boy stopped to lean against a stone wall, panting for breath.

How can I become a great matador, renowned throughout Spain, he thought, *unless I practice?*

He enjoyed a brief moment of indignation, before fear clouded his dreams of glory. *Will father learn of my adventure? Will I be punished?* He dashed home.

* * *

Gaspar shivered in the cold hall, rubbed his hands together, and continued to write. Despite the chill, he liked the hushed library chamber, his classmates around him, heads bent over books, the scritch, scratch of pens on paper.

Books, writing, study, he was in his element, comfortable and happy. This morning, however, he could not keep his mind from drifting, could not attend to his work, even as important exams approached, he was unable to concentrate.

I must do well, he thought. *If I am successful, I will, no doubt, be sent to Alcalá de Henares to complete my studies at the University...I will be near Madrid...I must keep my mind on my work.*

Even as he encouraged himself, the words on the page blurred before him. It was two years ago, and he was on the road again, the lurching mule-drawn coach leaving Oviedo behind on its way to Avila. The green hills of Asturias, its beautiful trees and woodlands, the geometric shapes of planted fields in manmade harmony with nature had given way to the dry, flat, barren lands of the Meseta.

"Ahem!' the rector cleared his throat.

Gaspar pushed his nose closer to his book. "Principles of Canon Law" he read, but in his mind he saw farmers toiling under a hot sun, oxen, plows.

How hard they work, he thought, *and how dry the farms seem. They need irrigation.*

"Ahem!"

Gaspar tapped his foot quietly on the stone floor, reined in his wandering thoughts, and picking up his pen, began to write. A movement to his left, however, distracted him, and he turned toward a corner of the library to see a woman on hands and knees, scrubbing the floor. The boy's eyes followed her as she progressed slowly, pushing a bucket ahead of her scrubbing brush.

Watching her, Gaspar's mind was home again in the comfortable Jovellanos house with his elegant, refined mother and his four lovely, well-educated sisters. He saw his eldest sister Benita's face, remembered her kindness and love of learning.

His eyes fixed on the laboring woman, he thought, *I wonder if she can read?*

Tap! Tap! Tap! The rector's pointer stick rapped the podium. "Jovellanos!"

Gaspar ducked his nose down toward his papers.

Francisco de Goya raised his schoolbook to conceal most of his face and whispered to his friend on the bench beside him.

"I am going to art school, Martín. My father has arranged to send me. I will learn to mix colors and to paint with oils."

"That is good, Francisco," his friend whispered back, "Then everyone will be happy. You will not have to draw all over the walls, and you will not be running around like a wild thing." He tried to keep from laughing and instead snorted loudly.

A warning tap-tap-tap from the teacher's rod, and a stern, "Zapater! Goya!" silenced the boys.

"I will miss you," Martín mouthed the words.

"I will always be your friend," Francisco whispered back.

Tap-Tap-Tap!

* * *

At twenty years, Gaspar had grown tall and hand-some. Slim and agile, he held his head high. His dark eyes glistened with warmth and kindness.

At Alcalá de Henares, he stood before Juan Arias de Saavedra, a highly esteemed agent from Madrid, who conducted oral examinations and offered opinions on career placements for the University's students.

Saavedra was strongly-built, his dark hair flecked with gray. A beard, running along his jaw, met the droop of his mustache. His eyes, dark and quietly penetrating, looked a long moment at the young man standing before him before he began his questions.

"Gaspar Jovellanos," the voice was firm, forceful, yet amiable. "What is it that seems most important to you and to your life's work?" Saavedra waited, staring calmly at the young student.

"To seek the truth," Gaspar began tentatively, "to bring light where there is darkness." He paused to think a mo-ment, before letting his agreeable voice fill the chamber more confidently, "To help the unfortunate, to improve their lives, and to end their misery." He paused again, this time to breathe.

"To treat my fellow human beings with the respect they deserve as God's creation," he continued, his thoughts com-ing rapidly now, "to establish order where there is chaos, to provide education, yes, to educate my countrymen and, thus, to guarantee the well being of my country." Gaspar exhaled slowly.

Saavedra remained still, his dark eyes shining. Deeply impressed by the young scholar's personal qualities, his brilliant mind, his education, his hope of being useful to his fellow men and to his country, the agent's mind worked quickly. He would undertake the task of convincing the young genius he recognized before him that, rather than the ministry, he was better suited for a career in service to his country. That accomplished, he would write at once to inform the bishop of the change in plans.

Thus, after years of study, Gaspar returned home to Gijón, to his beloved hills and trees and seashore. He was embraced joyously, lovingly by his parents and surrounded again by the warmth of family and friends. His stay in Asturias would be temporary, however. His new position as criminal magistrate awaited him. Before long he would travel south to Andalusia.

Francisco de Goya had met Ramón Bayeu in José Luzán's art studio where they had studied, worked together, and become friends. He had learned his craft during his years with Luzán, mixing colors, drawing, working in oils, learning the fresco technique of applying color to wet plaster.

Ramón had a pretty sister, Josefa, and a brother, Francisco, who painted in Madrid and had important connections in the city. Goya, from humble beginnings, had no connections, only talent and ambition. He had come to Madrid in his late teens, to continue to learn and to perfect his style, had applied to the prestigious Royal Academy of Fine Arts and been rejected.

Now he stood in the blaze of a July sun painting in public next to Ramón. Both had applied for admission to the

Academy, Goya for the second time. They had two and a half hours to complete their paintings.

His dark, curly hair matted against his forehead, perspiration trickled down Goya's brow and over his face. He wiped a bare arm over his intense and focused eyes. His brush worked feverishly.

When he had finished, he waited for the judges, including Francisco Bayeu, Painter to the King and influential in the Academy, to view the artwork and to hear the results:

"Ramón Bayeu has won First Prize!"

Not one vote, Goya realized, *I did not receive one vote.* He stood in the sun, his mouth dry, swallowing hard, his stomach a lump of coarse gravel.

Deeply discouraged, he thought, *Francisco Bayeu has offered me a job as an assistant. Perhaps I should accept.* His restless spirit, however, would not accept defeat. *No, not yet,* he decided. Italy, the mecca of artists beckoned to him. *I will go adventuring and view the paintings of the Italian Masters, Michelangelo and Raffaello.*

He planned to live inexpensively and remain a long time. He was not sure when he would see Spain again.

CHAPTER TWO
South to Seville

Bouncing along a dirt road, Gaspar looked through a small coach window at the violet-gray hills of the Sierra Morena on the horizon. Rumbling to the left, the coach lurched over a patch of rough road. He steadied himself against the door and caught the first glimpse of his new city.

Seville, shimmering under a dazzling southern sun, was a burst of brilliance against the green Andalusian countryside. Here was the city from which King Ferdinand and Queen Isabella had sent Colon on his voyage to the New World.

Gaspar watched the city grow closer, its golden glow drawing him forward until it surrounded him, welcomed him. The coach jostled its way over cobblestones, stopping finally in a last bone-shaking jolt. Stepping from the coach, he paused to stretch his cramped legs before dispatching his bags to his new residence.

I'll take a little time to explore my new city, he thought and walked along, intrigued by its maze of alleys and small streets and enjoying the bustle of the busy *Sevillanos*. Turning into a crowded alley, he saw a small boy sitting on the ground near a wall, bare legs bent beneath him and brown pants ragged about his knees. *Poor boy*, he thought, watching the child inspect his worn jacket and pick fleas from his bare chest.

Gaspar continued to walk, lost in thought, remembering his own happy childhood in Gijón. Before long, he stood on a quiet street before a two-story stone house, which Juan Arias de Saavedra had arranged for his lodging. Moving through the arched portal into a cool, dim passage, he proceeded toward the light at the end of the corridor.

The house, Roman in design, had a central courtyard surrounded by small rooms. In one, the library, he saw neat stacks of his books and papers.

The patio revealed a waterless, stone fountain, two small palm trees, and a few straggly, unattended shrubs. Empty terra cotta pots stood stacked against a wall. A lonesome aura permeated the deserted house, and Gaspar was standing thoughtfully in the silent courtyard, when footsteps in the corridor drew his attention.

"So you have arrived," a warm, animated voice broke through his thoughts, "Welcome, *señor* Jovellanos! Welcome to Seville!"

Gaspar turned to stare into the dark eyes and smiling face of a tall, elegantly dressed man in the courtyard doorway.

"I am Pablo de Olavide, governor of this enchanting city," he extended his hand, "I trust your journey was comfortable. Saavedra has written to me of your arrival. Please feel free to bring any of your needs to me."

"*Gracias*," Gaspar answered, returning the firm handshake.

"A servant will arrive tomorrow to assist you," Olavide continued in high spirits. "Tonight, I would request the pleasure of your company at my home for dinner. We can discuss the affairs of Asturias as well as the needs of Seville." He extended a small card to Gaspar. "Nine o'clock then. My home is not far from here. A pleasant walk. *Hasta luego.*"

*   *   *

The next morning, Gaspar awakened to light sifting through a shuttered window. The patio was already warming under the early sun.

Thankfully, he reflected, *the house's thick walls and tiled roof cool the inner rooms.*

He sighed, thinking ahead to his first day as magistrate of criminal justice in Seville's municipal government, a position not particularly appealing to his amiable nature.

I'm not sure that I'm the right man for this job, he thought, *but it is my first post, and I will endeavor to do my best.*

Walking to his office, while the city awakened around him, Gaspar reflected on his visit to the home of Pablo de Olavide. During dinner, the men had engaged in a lively discussion of literature, philosophy, and politics. The evening had passed pleasantly for Gaspar, who enjoyed sharing ideas, especially on the need for reforms and progress in Spain.

He had accepted happily the man's invitation to use his library and had noted that the collection contained many foreign works. In addition to Castellano and Latin, Gaspar knew French and Italian. He planned during his stay in Seville to learn English as well.

Today, however, he thought, *I must visit the city's prison.*

CHAPTER THREE
A Prison and Paintings

Descending the narrow, circular stairway in the cool, dank air, Gaspar grew increasingly aware of a stench which seemed to permeate the stained and damply-oozing stones of the prison walls. Endeavoring to maintain his composure, he kept his face expressionless

He paused before a cell door. The grizzled face of a hunched man, his mouth hanging open, gaped at him through the bars of the small enclosure. Gaps separated coffee-colored teeth, and a torn shirt revealed a gaunt, ribbed chest.

Gaspar stood facing the man a moment before moving on to the other cells. In each, he saw confined individuals. Some lay on the hard floor, others stood hunched over, glaring.

"What crimes have these people committed?" he asked the guard accompanying him, a middle-aged man, rotund, and red-faced.

"A great variety, *señor*. Some await trials for a long time. Some will go before the courts of the Inquisition."

Outside in the open air, Gaspar lifted his face to the sun and breathed deeply to refresh his lungs. *Why did I accept this position?* he wondered. *What can I do here? I have no talent for this work. What can I possibly do?*

He needed to walk. It was his habit to enjoy daily *paseos*, usually in the early morning or late afternoon, with a friend to share ideas or alone to clear his head and to sort his thoughts. Now, as high noon approached, he walked alone, dazzled by the sudden rush of light on his eyes accustomed to the dark prison.

Moving through the blaze of sun, he sensed that this day's walk would neither clear his thoughts nor erase the growing feeling of hopelessness he had for his new job. He walked somewhat unsteadily down an empty street, as the *Sevillanos* sought shade and coolness indoors.

Feeling the heat, Gaspar turned into an open church doorway. From the dim foyer, he glanced down the main aisle to a gilded and ornately-decorated altar. The church glowed softly with the light from flickering candles. Moving into the cool interior, the dazzle of the street behind him, all was suddenly quiet, tranquil.

Halfway down the main aisle, he turned right toward a small sanctuary and gazing at the painting above the side altar, halted, startled by the scene before him. Beautiful natural figures, limbs, and faces caressed by warm light, Spanish faces, handsome faces.

"Everything in the composition seems natural and real," Gaspar whispered admiringly, studying the painting's details. "The father rejoices at the return of his lost son. It is a biblical scene rendered fresh and new.

"Murillo," he said softly, recognizing the work's creator, "Bartolomé Esteban Murillo."

Gaspar had studied the lives and works of the great Sevillean painters, Velázquez and Murillo. Now he stood in silence, amid flickering lights, feeling the beauty and harmony of the painting wash over him, letting the color and forms of his gifted countryman soothe his soul.

At length, he turned to his left, and saw two paintings on an adjacent wall. Moving forward to gaze more closely at them, he recognized St. Elizabeth caring for the sick in a scene of compassion by the hand of the same artist, and in the other painting, a prison scene, St. Peter arrested, in chains, a glowing angel, swathed in light, extending a powerful arm to the weary, aging man, reviving him, setting him free.

Fascinated by Murillo's use of illumination in the painting, Gaspar murmured, thoughtfully, "Light penetrates darkness."

Deeply troubled by the demands of his new position and unsure of his abilities to cope with them, Gaspar stared a long time at the paintings.

CHAPTER FOUR
Elena

Alone in the tranquillity of his library, Gaspar began to write a report on prison reform. *Perhaps, there is something I can do after all*, he mused, before plunking his pen into the inkwell and beginning to scratch words onto paper.

Inspired by the compassionate brush of his countryman, Murillo, he worked quickly, writing freely, brainstorming ideas to elaborate later. His mind flowed with ideas for alleviating suffering and for treating individuals humanely. He argued against keeping prisoners awaiting trials for long periods of time, protested the placement of minor offenders with hardened criminals, urged the reform of squalid living conditions, and argued forcefully against using instruments of torture, demanding their elimination.

At length, he put down his pen. "I will review this tomorrow and then dispatch it to Madrid," he said thoughtfully and relaxed back in his chair.

His servant approached with a note from Olavide inviting him to dine the following evening and to converse with guests from the university city of Salamanca.

*   *   *

Gaspar walked to the home of Olavide, gave his hat to the doorman, and proceeded to the drawing room, a bustle of conversation and laughter growing steadily louder as he approached the gathering.

"Good Evening, my friend," Olavide smiled warmly, turning from a conversation and extending a hand to him. "May I introduce to you Javier Echevarria." Gaspar shook hands with a gray-haired, portly man. The gentleman, one of the wealthiest in Seville, was slightly bent and leaned heavily on a carved walking stick. He had a long, beaked nose, and his small, shrewd eyes peered from a round, flat face. He nodded to Gaspar and smiled.

"Come, there are several people that I would like you to meet," Olavide continued, "They are writers from Salamanca."

Gaspar was soon deep in conversation with the men, sharing thoughts on poetry and drama as well as criminal justice reform. Olavide poured wine for his guests and moved among them in the candlelit room, listening, now and then engaging in conversation.

Gaspar relished the discussions and exchange of ideas. Glancing about, he noticed ladies in the room, wives of the gentlemen guests, chatting together in a group. Fashionably dressed, their silk skirts rustled pleasantly as they moved. Ribbons and lace ornamented curls piled on heads. They held fans, ornate lacy folds, and waved them slowly, languidly as they chatted.

"*Señor* Jovellanos, I would like to introduce to you Alejandro Suarez, an associate of Echevarria." Olavide's voice was behind him. Gaspar turned, smiling, to face Olavide and a tall, slim man at his side. He nodded, shaking the older gentleman's hand. "And his daughter, Elena," his host continued the introductions.

Moving from behind her father, the young woman appeared quietly at his side. She looked calmly into Gaspar's dark, thoughtful eyes and smiled.

The young Asturian felt an inward jab that seemed to expand upward to his lungs. He caught his breath, stared into her warm, black eyes and nodded, unable, for the moment, to speak. From somewhere distant, he heard Olavide's amused voice explaining the Suarez agricultural holdings and the girl's accomplishments in art and music.

Gaspar tried to attend to his friend's words but saw only dark ringlets of hair adorned with flowers, a pearly complexion, rosy lips, and delicate, silvery lace over slim shoulders. To save his life, he could not speak a word.

Suarez's cool, haughty voice filled the silence. "Pablo has told me of your ideas on agricultural reform and land use. Perhaps you would do me the pleasure of visiting my home, of dining with my family and me, to share your thoughts on these matters?"

Gaspar, recovering at last, accepted the invitation. His wits returning, he reclaimed his composure and elegant demeanor. He bowed to the gentleman and to his strikingly beautiful daughter.

"It is my pleasure to have met you," he said, "and I look forward to seeing you again." For a moment, his eyes met the girl's gaze. He nodded quickly and turned toward the nearest group of men.

Gaspar tried to regain his place in the conversation, but his attention wavered and, more than once, he stole a glance at the girl, who had moved with her father, to the opposite side of the room to join another circle of guests.

From a distance, he completed his appraisal of her. Medium height, slim, an elegant air, her smile seemed like sunshine and her laughter ripples of music.

He walked home under a brilliant Andalusian moon. The evening had been fraught with topics to stimulate and to satisfy his active, intelligent mind, and during the evening, Gaspar had reveled in the exchange of ideas. At the moment, however, he could remember little of what he had discussed at the house of Olavide.

Easy, my boy, he chuckled to himself. *Get yourself together. You cannot allow a beautiful head of curls to muddle you.*

Grinning for no reason in particular and humming as he entered his house, he called out a cheery greeting to his amazed and startled servant.

CHAPTER FIVE
An Untamed Spirit

The Suarez patio was lush with trees and flowering bushes. Classical archways and elegant, fluted columns surrounded the greenery. In the center, a fountain spilled water from a bucket held by the statue of a slim, bronze boy, half-real, half-godlike.

A Roman youth, Gaspar mused, enjoying the Renaissance feel of the enclosure's design and noting the statue's tunic and toga.

Spanish roses cascaded over a wall while wisteria vines clung to one another. Close to the fountain jasmine blossoms scented the evening air.

Earlier, the sweet fragrance had found its way from the garden to Gaspar in the dining room. Now, with Elena by his side, he stood in the patio. Candlelight from doors opened to the courtyard softly illumined the darkness. The fountain gurgled gently.

He was aware of Elena's hand on his arm. Since their first meeting months ago, his reputation for intelligence and honesty had spread, gaining the attention of the girl's family, and affording him opportunities to spend time with her. They had strolled often together in the late afternoon sharing conversation and had attended evenings at the home of Olavide. As his friendships deepened, not only with the writers from Salamanca, but with the progressive thinkers and reformers of Seville, Gaspar had invited guests to his own home.

The dinner with the Suarez family had proceeded pleasantly, if a bit slowly for Gaspar. With much on his mind and eager to speak with Elena, he had waited patiently until they could share a moment alone. Considerable thought and planning had prepared him for what he would say to her.

Now, in the candle glow, the fragrance of jasmine heavy around him, his thoughts went fuzzy. He could feel his heart thumping. She was beautiful, sweet, intelligent, and the deep, dark eyes gazing back at him were warm.

Gaspar breathed deeply and plunged ahead.

"Elena," he said. She answered with a sweet smile, and his words caught in his throat.

"Elena," he began again, smiling gently. "I am leaving Seville."

Her hand tightened on his arm.

"I am going to Madrid," he continued rapidly. "I have received an appointment as magistrate. It is an excellent opportunity for me, a chance to work more closely with the King and his government."

Gaspar saw that her lower lip trembled. When she tried to turn from him, he took her hand from his arm and grasped it firmly between both of his. She averted her face.

Gaspar continued undaunted, determined, speaking to the girl's profile. "Elena, before I move to Madrid, I must take a short trip south, a few weeks, to inspect and report on farming and land usage near Jerez de la Frontera.

When I return, if you consent, I will ask your father for your hand."

She turned suddenly toward him, her face flushed with pleasure. His heart skipped a beat, and he gulped before continuing.

"Elena, the Jovellanos family is old and noble, but we have always worked for our livelihoods. I cannot promise you great wealth, only my humble heart," he hesitated. "Will you be my wife?"

"*Sí*, Gaspar, *Sí*," she said eagerly, without hesitation. Stepping closer to him, she pressed her cheek against the hands grasping hers.

Gaspar's heart swelled. He freed one hand and raising it to her head, caressed the curls he found there. Elena moved against his chest, and Gaspar, wrapping his arms around her, held her close to him.

*   *   *

The carriage drive to Jerez de la Frontera carried Gaspar through the Andalusian countryside. As days went by, he became familiar with the farmland, *haciendas*, orchards, and irrigation techniques of the area.

Filled with energy and feeling a zest in his limbs, a vigor he had never before realized, everything in life seemed promising. Olavide and the gentlemen from Salamanca had encouraged him to write, and his mind was full of ideas for poems and drama. He would continue writing in Madrid, and with Elena by his side, would host brilliant gatherings attended by the best minds in the Capital.

Such were his thoughts, as he reached the last stop in his fact-finding journey. Jerez de la Frontera was not far from the Atlantic coast. Through the centuries the city had hosted and experienced Romans, Visigoths, and Moors. A crossroads for commerce, it was well known for its trade in horses.

Weary after many miles of travel, Gaspar planned to spend several days in Jerez writing his report before returning to Seville. Arriving at an inn where he would pass the interlude, he enjoyed a light meal and a brief *siesta*, before taking his daily *paseo*, leisurely walking through the streets of the pleasant city.

His steps took him to the corrals at the heart of the market area. Like all of the Jovellanos before him, Gaspar was an able horseman with an eye for fine animals. He approached a sandy arena surrounded by prospective buyers and found a seat on a wooden bench partially shaded by an oak tree.

Andalusian horses, strong, beautiful, and swift, were often sold at the Jerez market. The exceptional animals were famous for their intelligence and gentleness.

Magnificent, he thought, as the horses pranced before him. He noted their beautifully shaped, intelligent heads and long legs built for speed and endurance. *And costly*, he continued to himself.

"Fine horses, fit for a king, *señor*."

Gaspar turned to look into the grinning face of a young man and acknowledged the amiable smile with a nod, before returning his attention to the arena. The youth wore black breeches and a short, black jacket. A ruffled collar tied at the neck and a black hat at a jaunty angle completed his costume. Still grinning, he eyed Gaspar, noting his easy, relaxed manner, intelligent face, the cut of his clothes.

"If you are looking for a horse, *señor*, that black would do you proud in any of our fine cities, even at the Royal Palace in Madrid."

Gaspar had not come to Jerez to purchase a horse.

"Just looking," he replied.

"The best horses come here to Jerez from the farms of Spain and beyond, but our Andalusians, cannot be surpassed for speed, stamina, and heart."

Gaspar nodded his agreement but did not reply. His attention was drawn to a stallion entering the corral.

A beautiful, gray Andalusian, he thought, *with all the admirable characteristics of the breed.*

To Gaspar's surprise, the horse suddenly balked and pulled its head back sharply as a groom struggled to control him. Snorting, it yanked its head viciously against the rein. Rearing on hind legs, its hooves pawed the air.

"That one," the young man beside Gaspar commented, "*es un diablo*. He will not be controlled. It is tragic, a useless creature."

Amazed, Gaspar watched the ferocious struggle between groom and horse. The animal, large and powerfully built, was perhaps a year or two old. His appearance testified to his excellent breeding and lineage, yet his behavior was uncharacteristic of the famously gentle Andalusian. Gaspar admired spirit in a horse, but this *caballo* was angry and violent.

What has caused this in you? he wondered, watching the creature struggling against the rein.

Suddenly, he had his answer. From the side of the corral, a short, rotund man, well-dressed in black, a red satin sash wound around his ample girth, moved toward the horse. A long switch in hand, he began to snap it against the animal. The horse's ferocity increased under the torment. Horrified by the spectacle, Gaspar sat motionless, frozen.

"He wants to show how he can be controlled," his companion muttered, his voice tinged with disgust. "That one wants him sold, but who will want to buy a disaster like that?"

✳   ✳   ✳

In the coolness of early twilight, Gaspar walked slowly back to the inn. Aware of the strain in his right arm, he focused his attention forward and ignored the glances of passersby.

He had thought, perhaps, of purchasing a horse in Madrid, a horse to pull a carriage, a well-mannered animal to please Elena. He had not intended to buy one in Jerez.

He pressed his arm firmly against his body to prevent it from being yanked backward and led the great, gray, snorting, prancing animal toward the inn. Ignoring the young groom's frightened eyes, he secured a stall for the horse in the adjoining stable.

Once inside the enclosure, the animal moved restlessly in the small space, shook its head, kicked, and in general disturbed the peace of his stablemates.

The groom refusing to go near the stall, Gaspar filled the trough with water and forked hay to the animal.

"He will want oats later," he told the young fellow. "I will return to feed him."

He stood for a moment contemplating his new possession, the beautifully shaped head, the deep gray coat, the silvery tones of the mane and tail. The horse, settled for a moment, head lowered, sides heaving, and looked back at its new master.

"What shall I call you?" Gaspar spoke quietly, soothingly. "Perhaps *Gris* for your color. Hmmm, would you like that?"

The horse, motionless a moment, extended its neck, whinnied loudly and kicked the back wall of the stall.

"Well," Gaspar grinned, "perhaps *Diablo* may be more suitable."

Having exchanged a good part of his salary for the horse, he mused, *I am a rational man, who has made an irrational purchase.*

Gaspar spent the final days in Jerez visiting the countryside and completing his report. Each day, he visited his new acquisition, feeding and, as always, speaking softly and soothingly to the animal. Leading the horse around the corral for exercise proved a considerable challenge, and Gaspar's right arm was often sore.

His efforts to calm the horse a failure, he departed Jerez for Seville, his bags and newly purchased saddle gear stowed atop the coach, while behind and tethered to the vehicle, a semi-wild, gray stallion pranced.

Through the coach window, Gaspar watched the passing countryside, and with each mile, his excitement and happiness increased, as he anticipated his return to his beloved, Elena.

CHAPTER SIX
Onward!

Seville was slumbering in late afternoon heat when Gaspar arrived home. His servant stared wide-eyed as his dignified master settled a highly irritated horse into the small stable behind the dwelling.

Later that night, relaxed in a large copper tub, the hot water easing his weariness, Gaspar rehearsed his words to Elena's father.

"I will go to Madrid and find a house. Your family will have time to prepare for the wedding. Afterwards, Elena and I will return to Madrid to begin our lives together."

Gaspar slept well and not long after dawn made his way to the Suarez home. He inhaled the fresh air of Seville's morning. His eagerness pulsed in his veins, and he quickened his step.

A canopy of palm trees shaded the approach to the residence, and two cypress trees, symbols of welcome, flanked the front portal. Gaspar tapped the metal knocker against the large, sturdy wooden door and waited a few moments before knocking again, this time allowing the rapper to fall more heavily upon the wood. Again, he waited. Slowly, a small slat slid aside, and Gaspar saw the eyes of a servant peering at him.

"Gaspar Jovellanos to see *el señor* Suarez, *por favor.*"

The eyes widened. Gaspar began to feel bewildered.

"I wish to speak with *el señor* Suarez, please," he repeated.

"*El señor no está*," the servant replied hurriedly. He began to replace the slat.

"*Un momento, por favor*," Gaspar interjected. "I wish to see *la señorita*."

The slat slammed shut in his startled face. Reaching for the knocker, he paused, feeling a hand on his shoulder, and turning quickly, looked into the serious face of Pablo de Olavide.

"She is gone, Gaspar," his friend said softly. "She left several days ago."

"Where? Why?" Gaspar asked.

"Her father agreed to her betrothal to Javier Echevarria. He is a wealthy man, Gaspar, and she will live in luxury, like a queen. It was her father's wish, and she consented."

Gaspar, shocked and repulsed, struggled to control himself.

"How can this be?" he muttered, his words sluggish. "She agreed to marry me."

"Gaspar, I missed you at home by minutes this morning," Olavide continued, wounded by the pain he saw in his young friend's face. "I wanted to explain." He cast about for words. "Suarez was aware of your growing attachment to his daughter and of her affection for you," he said, struggling to speak calmly. "He was also aware of your financial status. He made a business decision. It happens all too often, my friend."

Gaspar felt his face go hot and anger well within him. "Echevarria is an old man," he replied, struggling not to be sick, his breath coming in short gasps. "I have to find her and save her," he said suddenly. "Where is she? I have to hurry."

Olavide looked Gaspar squarely in the face. "Gaspar, they are married."

Seeing his friend's distress at these words, Olavide reached his hand to grasp his shoulder, but Gaspar pulled back and turning to leave, stumbled away from the house, leaving behind him his dreams and his love.

He walked dazedly through streets filling with people he did not see. *What evil is this?* he thought. His beautiful, young love given to an old man for money, to live like a queen. Olavide's voice echoed in his brain, *It happens often...a business deal.*

Two days later, a small coach carrying a lady and three gentlemen departed Seville in the early hours before dawn. A team of mules pulled it eastward along the Guadalquivir River through Andalusia along a route toward Castile and La Mancha and, finally, Madrid. A gray stallion pranced behind the vehicle, its high spirits in stark contrast to those of its master within the coach.

※　　※　　※

Francisco's days among the Italians slipped by pleasantly. There was much for him to see and to do in the country's sunny ambiance.

"Artwork seems everywhere," he wrote to Martin Zapater. "Sculptures, paintings, even the delightful gardens and the people themselves do much to inspire me."

He decided to enter another contest, one offered by the Academy of Fine Arts in Parma, and completed and

submitted his entry. Again he waited for the judges to announce the winners.

First prize went to an Italian painter, and second prize
to the young Spanish artist. Goya beamed with pride, glowing in the praise heaped on him by the highly-respected
Italian judges and from a French newspaper as well.

It was time to go home, time to court the lovely Josefa
Bayeu. Their marriage, he was aware, would connect him
to an important and influential family. It was time, also,
to accept the position in Madrid offered to him through
Francisco Bayeu in the King's Tapestry Factory. He would
paint scenes of Spanish life to be reproduced in silk and
wool woven into tapestries for the walls of royal buildings.
With his prestigious prize in hand, it was time for Francisco de Goya to go home to Spain.

CHAPTER SEVEN
An Accident

The coach following the Guadalquivir River turned northward into the Sierra Morena, and snaked its way around hills, stopping from time to time to afford its occupants refreshment and relaxation.

As the journey progressed, Gaspar's appetite returned, as well as his appreciation of the landscapes and vegetation through which he passed. At first reluctant to talk with his companions, he gradually recovered his natural amiability and good manners. The dark eyes a bit more brooding, the elegant demeanor somewhat aloof, and a dull ache deep within, his memories of the last days in Seville, nevertheless, faded with each mile.

He cared well for his great, gray horse, watering, feeding, and attending to it personally from necessity since no one would go near it. Gaspar, however, found that he enjoyed looking after the animal and often chatted with it.

"It is a long walk, gray one," he spoke calmly, quietly, "but we are seeing the landscapes of our beautiful country. Soon we will reach Madrid."

In response, the horse rolled its eyes, snorted, and pawed the ground.

"Some men try to destroy the spirit in others because they have none of their own," he continued to the animal. "Is that what happened to you, *caballo*? Is that why you have such an unfriendly attitude?"

The horse snorted again, flicked back its ears, and pulled against its tether.

"I see that we are becoming great friends," his master grinned.

The days continued peacefully along the road to Madrid. One afternoon, however, passing through a small wooded glen, the coach moved at an excessive speed, and rounding a bend, the coachman too late saw a log jutting into the path. One wheel jolted over the log, tilting the coach at a precarious angle, and the mules, lurching forward, snapped their harness straps. Seated at a window, Gaspar saw the earth rush up, and with a smashing crash, all was darkness.

Flung from his seat, he lay sprawled on the coach door. He attempted to sit up, but lay back with a small grunt of pain, his right temple throbbing.

"Are you all right, *señor*?" One of the passengers called to him from outside the coach.

"Yes," he answered, despite the pain, "I'm fine."

Struggling again to pull himself upright, he reached for the door above him and with a deep breath, hoisted himself through the opening.

Sitting atop the overturned coach inspecting his badly-scraped right shin, he was relieved that, aside from his aching head and bloodied leg, he had escaped the upset without serious injury. Climbing down from the coach, he tore a strip from his shirt and wrapped it around his leg.

Somewhat dazed, Gaspar looked about to see if the other passengers needed assistance. He spied them walking slowly toward a large tree with the coachman and his attendant. All were bruised and bloodied. The team of mules had disappeared down the road.

Wondering what to do next, Gaspar heard voices and the rattle of an approaching wagon. "Ah," he sighed in relief, "help is coming."

In a short time, several men from a nearby village, alerted by the runaway mule team, arrived at the accident scene. If he thought that they had come to help all of the injured, Gaspar was surprisingly mistaken. On the contrary, ignoring the well-dressed passengers, the men attended only to the coachman and his helper and assisted them into the wagon. To Gaspar's amazement and dismay, the passengers, including the woman, were obliged to follow the wagon on foot down the village road.

"They help their equals, not those they perceive as nobility," he mused quietly. Suddenly, startled from his thoughts, his brain clearing, he whirled and walked to the coach as quickly as his injured leg allowed. Fingering the broken tether strap still attached to the vehicle, Gaspar glanced about the deserted, silent scene. A soft breeze moved through the trees. Beyond them, he saw open fields stretching to the horizon.

"Well, my friend," he said wistfully, "you have found your freedom from all who have tormented you."

Turning from the coach, a familiar sound startled him. He paused, looked toward the sound, and noticed a small space among the trees and underbrush. He heard it again...a snort. Limping into the clearing, he stopped as man and horse faced each other.

"*Amigo*, you are free at last," Gaspar said in his quiet voice. "Go on, run, and throw your demons to the wind. *Adiós*, gray one."

His head and injured leg throbbing, he turned away. "I had better start walking to the village before dark or spend the night here," he said to himself, not happy with either choice.

He took a few painful steps and stopped. Something soft and warm was near his neck. Slowly, Gaspar turned his aching head toward his left shoulder, felt the horse's breath close to his face, and smiled in spite of his pain.

Slowly, carefully, he turned to the animal. The beautiful Spanish head very near to him, Gaspar slowly lifted his right hand, touched the soft muzzle, and reaching up carefully, stroked the forehead.

"You did not run away," he said gently.

The response, this time a quiet nicker, encouraged Gaspar to run his hand down the arched neck, across the powerful shoulder and shiny gray flank that quivered under his touch. He stroked and rubbed the horse's forehead again.

"I shall call you *Robles*, after the great, gray oaks of Asturias. They are strong like you and beautiful."

In the gathering twilight, the horse followed him from the clearing. Reflecting a moment, Gaspar walked to the overturned coach and rustled through the bags in the cargo space.

Robles accepted the bit and chewed it quietly, nodding his head and flicking his silvery tail, as the saddle was placed carefully on his back and cinched firmly.

Gaspar, relieved that the bridle and saddle were familiar to the horse, took the reins in hand and stood beside the magnificent Andalusian. Although an expert horseman, he was keenly aware of his less than perfect physical condition, and the thought of being tossed to the ground from an irritated horse did not especially appeal to him.

"Well, my boy," he said at length, taking a deep breath, "here's to risks and great adventures!"

With that, he placed his foot in the stirrup and mounted quickly. He sat a moment, awaiting the consequences. When none came, he drew up the reins, clicked his tongue, and with a soft nudge of his knees, felt the great horse move forward quickly, energetically.

"Easy, Robles," Gaspar's voice soothed. "Take it easy on your master until the pain goes."

The horse settled into a walk. The village seemed closer now.

CHAPTER EIGHT
Windmills and a Horrible Cone

ays later riding northward, Gaspar reached a village and stopped for water at a small, stone well. While Robles satisfied his thirst at a trough, his master lounged on the grass nearby, watching a group of young boys playing in a field across the road.

One sat on the shoulders of another while a third struggled to stand under the weight of a rather plump friend. They shouted and laughed, the boys on top pushing and pulling at each other, pretending to be giants.

Gaspar, his billowy, white shirt opened at the neck, smiled at their antics and their exuberant voices. Nearby, some women seated at the roadside displayed pots and crockery for sale as a coach rattled by them.

Gaspar drank from his water skin, squeezing the bag, aiming the stream of liquid carefully into his mouth, before replenishing the skin at the well.

"Time to get going," he said, patting Robles.

For several days, they followed a dirt trail beaten smooth by coaches, horsemen, and herders. One evening, as the setting sun touched the horizon, spreading long golden rays across fields of grain and grass, they paused at the crest of a small rise.

"Look, Robles," Gaspar grinned. Ahead, on the rim of a hill, three large, white-stuccoed windmills turned brown, canvas arms lazily in a gentle breeze.

Gaspar leaned forward and stroked the horse's neck. "Do you know where we are, boy?" he asked, smiling happily. "This is the land of Cervantes."

Robles, eager to be on his way, bobbed his head and pranced a few sideways steps, but Gaspar drew him up and dismounted. Holding the reins with one hand, he stroked the gray head and undaunted by the animal's inattention, continued his explanation.

"This is where the writer placed his Don Quixote, his great knight...an old man, Robles, who wanted to right all the evils in the land. He was a dreamer...," Gaspar paused, his eyes faraway. "...He wanted things to be better. Imagine that, my great one, he wanted things to change, and everyone thought he was mad."

He wiped his brow with the back of a shirtsleeve. "He saw the world with his own eyes. Do you see those windmills, Robles?" Gaspar pointed toward the horizon. "Quixote saw enemies, giants. He had to do battle with them. They were standing in his way."

The canvas arms turned, glowing golden in the Spanish sun. In a field not far from the windmills, a farmer making his way home followed an ox slowly along a furrow of earth.

Suddenly, Gaspar mounted, and Robles, anticipating action, resumed his prancing sidesteps. Gaspar pressed his knees, and the horse bolted forward down the sun-baked path.

Gaspar grinned, feeling the animal's strength beneath him. When the path evened, he loosened the reins, and let

Robles run. The great horse, sensing his master's exuber-
ance, stretched its neck and, hooves flying, pounded the
earth. In high spirits Gaspar tapped the brim of his hat as
he and Robles flew past the windmills.

The farmer, hearing the thunder before he saw the
horse and rider, pushed back his straw hat, and paused.
Squinting in the sun, he smiled at the gray stallion and his
rider passing in a swirl of golden dust.

Days later, the windmills well behind them, Gaspar
turned Robles into a path shaded by stands of ancient olive
trees. Remembering their wild dash past the windmills, he
grinned, patting the smooth neck.

"Robles, you are a fine Rocinante," he said referring
to Quixote's horse. "Perhaps when we reach Madrid," he
mused, "we, too, will have a chance to face giants and to
make some changes." He looked above at the feathery,
gray-green leaves of the old trees, their craggy, gnarled
branches reaching across the path like elderly fingers. "We
shall see."

*   *   *

One afternoon, pushing on toward Madrid and un-
comfortable in the heat of the day, Gaspar spied a
village ahead on a small rise of earth.

"We will find water there, Robles, and perhaps some
shade."

He had grown accustomed to talking to the horse and
grinned, watching the gray ears flick back and forth at the
sound of his voice.

At the outskirts of the town, while Robles drank from
a trough, Gaspar drew water from a well and washed trail
dust from his mouth and throat. He refilled the water skin
before splashing his face and rubbing the back of his neck

with the cool wetness. He was running his wet hands through his hair when a sound in the distance caught his ear.

"Voices," he murmured, "Many of them. I wonder what's happening."

He led Robles down the street toward the curious noise. At an intersection of narrow lanes, Gaspar caught his breath, stopping short at the scene before him.

"What a crowd!" he said in a low voice and felt his stomach go queasy.

A wagon drawn by two sweat-lathered mules was surrounded by people who shouted with scorn and contempt. In the wagon, a woman sat alone wearing on her head a large, white cone. Gaspar knew what the cone was, the *coroza* worn by those accused of offenses by the Office of the Inquisition.

Sickened by the spectacle and the crowd's taunts and insults, Gaspar stared at the woman under the *coroza* as the wagon rumbled past him. Chancing to glance in his direction, she met his gaze, and in that brief moment, he saw her humiliation and anguish. The crowd followed, shouting and jeering.

"What has she done? Gaspar wondered aloud. "What could be her crime?"

A voice beside him responded, "I think she had possession of the wrong books, foreign books and unacceptable."

Gaspar grimaced in disgust. "What will become of her?"

"After the trial, probably prison," the voice answered, before moving away after the crowd.

Gaspar watched the wagon proceed slowly, tortuously down the lane before leading Robles in the opposite direction.

"Is there no remedy for this?" he muttered. "This spectacle degrades everyone, the poor soul in the wagon and all who participate in it." He glanced down the lane again. "Here is something that must change," he said softly to the horse, "but it will be a very large giant for us to face."

The scene haunted Gaspar as he and Robles continued on toward Madrid. He endeavored to push aside his thoughts and to let the serenity of the Spanish countryside console him. Madrid lay ahead, the great city, his work, the Royal Court.

"I will need all of my energy."

CHAPTER NINE
The Capital

Gaspar entered the capital on a warm autumn afternoon to find Madrid's streets thronged with carriages, riders on horseback, and pedestrians. In the congestion, reins firmly in hand, he attempted to keep Robles to a walk. The animal, however, sensing the excitement and the tumult of the city, arched its neck and began to prance in a high-stepping, quick trot, its fine Andalusian lines catching the admiring attention of passersby.

Gaspar smiled at the horse's enthusiasm. "Do you prefer urban life to the rural, my boy?" he chuckled, as they proceeded through the bustling streets.

Riding toward the Puerta del Sol where several avenues converged, they paused before the Royal Palace. Robles, impatient to continue, bobbed his head and chewed the bit, while Gaspar surveyed the ornate facade of the residence of the Kings and Queens of Spain.

How long before I see the interior? he wondered.

Moving on, they turned from the main thoroughfare down a quieter side street, and losing his audience, Robles slowed to a walk while Gaspar surveyed his surroundings. The street was tree-lined and hushed.

They clip-clopped under a small iron archway onto a terrace before a two-story stone house. A servant, walking quickly from the front doorway, caught hold of the horse's bridle, as Gaspar dismounted.

"*Bienvenido, señor* Jovellanos," he bowed, a small man with a wrinkled, amiable face, his bald head shining in the sunlight. "I am Pedro."

Gaspar nodded, smiling warmly.

"*Gracias*," he replied. "My horse will need a comfortable stall and food."

"*Por cierto, señor*, of course," he bowed again. "The stable is at the rear of the house. It is small but ready for your animal."

"Are there other servants?" Gaspar asked, "A groom perhaps?"

"Only I, *señor*. I will see to your horse's care myself."

Gaspar nodded, satisfied with the arrangement. A servant was, indeed, a luxury for him.

"I will tend to your horse after I have shown you the house, *señor*."

"No, Pedro," Gaspar interrupted calmly. "Look after him first. I will see myself inside."

The servant, concealing whatever surprise Gaspar's request had caused him, led Robles around the side of the house.

Walking through the arched portal, Gaspar grinned as he stepped, for good luck, into his new home right-foot-first over the threshold, in the style of the Ancient Greeks.

The enlightened man allowing himself a little superstition, he grinned.

A cool, dim passageway led to a living area lined with shelves, where Gaspar noted happily his ever-increasing collection of books and papers, sent ahead of his departure from Seville, awaited him.

Two glass doors at the far wall revealed the house's well-tended inner courtyard and garden. Amid the flowers, small shrubs, and graceful trees, a fountain in the center trickled water from a small stone dish into a larger basin. A wooden stairway to the left of the patio led to the upper floor.

The road-weary traveler opened the door on the upstairs landing and stared in awe at the room before him. Sunshine streaming through open shutters revealed a large, carved wooden bed, a thickly stuffed mattress, two fluffed pillows, and white bedsheets. A small fire, a kettle of steaming water suspended above it, crackled in the fireplace.

A hot tub and a little rest on that very large mattress seemed to him an excellent idea. He walked to the window and looked out to a small fenced area next to the stable. Gaspar glimpsed a gray head peering over the stable half door, a clump of hay in its mouth.

*　　*　　*

Stirring, he breathed deeply, a gentle rapping on the door forcing him to open his eyes. He had slept soundly after his long journey through the countryside, and, for a moment, the soft mattress, the clean bedding bewildered him.

Where am I? he thought.

The room had darkened, the shutters closed against the evening sky, the hearth extinguished.

"Señor, perdón."

Hearing Pedro's voice, memory washed over him, and he roused himself awake.

"*Sí*, Pedro, come in." Gaspar raised himself on one arm.

"*Señor, perdón.*" Pedro repeated, entering the room, "you have a visitor. Juan Arias de Saavedra is here and wishes to speak with you if convenient."

Gaspar was on his feet at the mention of the name of his old friend and patron. It was Saavedra who had guided him from his youth. It was he who had found this house for him and sent Pedro from his own staff to assist him. Gaspar had come to love and admire Juan Arias as a second father.

Pedro held out his dressing gown and helped him into it.

"What time is it, Pedro? I had not intended to sleep so long."

"It is 7:30 in the evening, *señor.*"

Saavedra was standing in the drawing room scanning the bookshelves. Seeing Gaspar, he smiled broadly, and the two friends embraced.

Pedro built up the fire and poured cups of hot chocolate for the men sitting before the hearth. They had much to discuss, and Gaspar was grateful for the few hours of sleep. His brain felt rested and charged.

"You have heard about Olavide," Saavedra began. "The authorities of the Inquisition have taken exception with him. They object to his correspondence with French writers and to what they refer to as his 'appreciation of foreign ideas.' He has lost his position and property and been confined in a monastery."

Gaspar nodded, his dark, brooding eyes staring at the fire.

"The Inquisition is in its last days," he responded at length. "Its leaders no doubt consider their action against my distinguished friend as some sort of victory." He paused, his gaze drifting to the bookshelves, the volumes catching the firelight's glow. "They are frightened, Juan. All who have power worry when authority is questioned. They resist and grow defensive."

Saavedra held the cup to his lips. His eyes peered over the rim and watched Gaspar closely.

"Before I left Seville," the young man continued slowly, wondering if the dull ache would return with the mention of the city. It did not, he discovered, and his words continued, "I wrote a letter in defense of Olavide, of his character, his scholarship, and his accomplishments. Apparently, it had little effect since he has been suppressed."

Saavedra placed the cup on the small table beside him. "It did, however, bring your own name to the attention of the Inquisition," he said soberly, looking at his friend, a slight furrow between his eyes. "It would be wise, perhaps, to avoid making enemies in high places. You yourself realize the danger of upsetting those in authority."

Gaspar's dark eyes met the gaze of his benefactor and confidant. "He is my friend, Juan. I had to do something to try to help him."

It was Juan Arias's turn to gaze at the fire. "Take care, Gaspar, now that you are in the capital. You are much admired for your intelligence and accomplishments, and rightly so. There is, however, intrigue in the Court, and there are those who are self-seeking and of lesser abilities than you, who will be annoyed and threatened by a man of talent and integrity." He turned and looked directly at

Gaspar. "Jealousy is a part of man's condition, and like a snake, it can wait in the grass to bite you."

Gaspar leaned back in his chair and grinned at his friend. "Then I shall be on guard for these human snakes," he chuckled, "wherever they slither."

*   *   *

Rising early the next day, Gaspar met Pedro in the drawing room.

"*Buenos días, señor,*" he nodded to Gaspar, who returned his greeting and accepted the card extended to him. "Your breakfast awaits you, *señor*. Since it is a pleasant morning, I have placed it in the garden. If you would rather enjoy it inside..."

"No, no, Pedro." Gaspar looked up from the card. "The garden is fine. *Gracias.*"

He proceeded through the glass doors into the small courtyard, where Pedro had spread a white cloth over a small table, and sat enjoying the rustle of birds in the shrubbery and the trickle of the small fountain. It was, indeed, a pleasant morning.

Pedro brought warm bread and a fine orange marmalade to spread on it. He poured coffee into a cup and placed a small dish of orange slices beside it.

"Would *señor* care for anything else?" The little man stood, his head slightly inclined toward Gaspar.

"*No, gracias, Pedro. Es bastante y excelente. Muchas Gracias.*"

Bowing, Pedro returned to the house, and Gaspar looked again at the card.

So, he mused, *I have been invited this evening to the home of the esteemed public prosecutor, Pedro Rodríguez Campomanes.*

Lost in thought a moment, the words of Juan Arias flickering in his memory, Gaspar placed an orange slice in his mouth. Startled from his reverie by its sweetness, he finished off the fruit and his appetite awakened, proceeded to the thick, crusty bread, which he spread with marmalade and ate between gulps of strong coffee.

The morning sun filtered into the courtyard, dappling the stone floor. Gaspar, warm and satisfied from his simple breakfast, and happily anticipating new acquaintances and an evening of lively discussion, chuckled, "No snakes in the grass, I hope."

CHAPTER TEN
Jovellanos and Goya

From a cushioned seat in Saavedra's coach, Gaspar watched Madrid pass by in the night. Down the main avenue of poplars, the two-horse team clip-clopped past tree trunks encircled by late-blooming roses. The windows of the Campomanes house, a two-story, neo-classic building, glittered with candlelight, while the entry drive bustled with coaches depositing guests.

A chatter of voices reached Gaspar's ears as he stepped through the front portal, and a servant bowed and accepted his hat and gloves. He and Juan Arias, elegant in their evening attire, proceeded through wide doors into a ballroom. Candelabras on the walls and suspended from the high ceiling bathed the room in festive light, and Gaspar was aware of the swish of silk and satin gowns and the scent of gentlemen's pipes.

Campomanes, portly in a silk suit and bulging a bit over a wide sash, beamed with pleasure as he approached Gaspar and Juan Arias.

"*Bienvenidos*, gentlemen," he said heartily. "Welcome to my home. You honor me with your presence this evening." He clasped Saavedra's hand warmly and turned to Gaspar.

"*Señor* Jovellanos, it is a great pleasure to meet you. I am grateful for your correspondence from Seville. I very much enjoyed reading your reports and hope that you will share your intriguing thoughts with us this evening, not only your expertise on economics and commerce, but your literary pursuits as well." He smiled graciously, while his sharp eyes stared at Gaspar. "Your fame has preceded you to our capital, *señor* Jovellanos," he added quietly.

Gaspar met the man's gaze evenly. "*Gracias, señor*, I am happy to be here." He looked beyond his rotund host to a gentleman nearby, who watched him with interest. Campomanes turned in the direction of Gaspar's glance.

"Ah, permit me to introduce to you Francisco de Cabarrús, a banking wizard who has come from France to live with us and to help us modernize our great country." Completing the introduction, he excused himself, moving off through the crowd of chattering guests in his ballroom.

Cabarrús, dressed in a gold brocade suit, a white ruffled tie wrapped around his neck, and white stockings to his knees, was plump. His stomach prevented the buttoning of his jacket. His hair, powdered gray, framed a round face flushed from the heat of the room. Gaspar spoke to him in French.

"*Señor*, please," the gentleman protested, "it is your Castellano that I wish to hear. I am a Spaniard now, and I wish to speak my new language as beautifully as do you."

The two men chatted amiably for a time about banking and commerce. From the corner of his eye, however, Gaspar grew aware of another gentleman in the crowded room, who not only eyed him closely, but listened intently to his conversation.

When Cabarrús moved off into the crowd, Gaspar turned and looked into the eavesdropping gentleman's face, a round, fleshy face surrounded by curly, dark, somewhat unkempt hair and remarkable for the bright, piercing eyes that looked closely and deeply at him as if to see what lived on the inside. *Artist's eyes*, Gaspar thought.

"Gaspar," Saavedra's voice brimmed with enthusiasm, "may I present to you Francisco José Goya y Lucientes, painter."

The two men, shaking hands, looked each other directly in the eye. Gaspar smiled pleasantly, and the artist, slightly shorter and of medium build, nodded.

Art a favorite topic, Gaspar was eager to engage in conversation. "Are you painting portraits, *señor* Goya?" he began.

"I paint cartoons to be woven into tapestries and hung on the walls of the royal residences. They are mostly pleasant scenes of Spanish life. I do accept private commissions and do portraits as well."

The swish of satin and silk again, and a dark-haired, strikingly beautiful woman paused before the artist. She wore a white gown gathered at the waist with a red sash and bow and a red ribbon adorning thick, black hair, cascading in ringlets to her shoulders and back. Her skin was creamy, pearl white; she carried a black lace fan.

Goya provided introductions. "*Señora*, may I present to you Gaspar Jovellanos. *Señor*, my very dear friend, the Duchess of Alba."

Gaspar bowed, as the woman curtsied gracefully.

"I am very pleased to meet you, Duchess," he said politely.

"A pleasure, *señor*." Her brilliant, dark eyes stared directly into his a moment, before with a slight nod, she moved away through the crowd of guests.

Deep within Gaspar, a memory awakened, the scent of jasmine and the melody of a fountain. He shook his head and roused himself. The artist was speaking again, "She is, without doubt, one of the most beautiful women in Spain and gracious and generous as well."

Gaspar needed a change of air. "Will you excuse me, gentlemen?" He nodded to Juan Arias and to Goya and moving into the crowd, directed his steps toward the nearest doorway. He was halfway down a hallway, the noise of the ballroom receding behind him, when he realized he was not alone. The painter had followed him.

At the end of the hall, Gaspar found the Campomanes library, a medium-sized room lined with bookshelves, and stopped short in the doorway, arrested by a painting on the wall above the room's fireplace.

Entering, he and Goya gazed up at the artwork. The painting glowed with yellow-brown tones. An old man holding a glass. Near him a young boy with a water skin.

"They are Spanish workers," Goya explained, "but their faces have dignity and worth. Their creator has lavished his compassion on them, ennobling them."

"As only Diego de Silva Velázquez could do," Gaspar agreed. "The artist saw in these humble people what I have seen across Spain. Many of our countrymen work hard and long for little reward. Many are uneducated, unappreciated," he paused, before adding, "and many rich noblemen lead idle, useless lives."

Goya had turned to stare at Gaspar, who, having recovered from the jasmine, let his thoughts flow freely. "Spain is wealthy, but she is also poor. She is rich with gold from America, but her people do not share that wealth. It stays with a few or goes to Europe to buy the things that we ourselves do not produce." Gaspar drew his gaze from the painting. His memory flickered again, this time with the image of an overturned carriage. "When there is a vast separation between people, resentment can breed. There needs to be more opportunity for all. Education...Education is the answer."

Amazed at his new acquaintance's torrent of words and the emotion behind them, the artist's penetrating eyes glittered with interest.

"*Señor* Jovellanos, I would be honored if you would one day very soon visit my studio to view some of my work."

Gaspar smiled with pleasure. "I will look forward to that, *señor* Goya."

Returning to the ballroom, the artist still beside him, Gaspar found Juan Arias chatting with an elegantly dressed couple. His friend introduced the Duke and Duchess of Osuna, also acquaintances of Goya.

The Duke, smiling pleasantly, bowed, while his wife gave her hand to Gaspar, who touched it lightly with his lips. Tall, slender, her hair powdered in a gray frizzle of curls about a thin face, she eyed him unblinking. She wore a gray satin gown adorned with jeweled buttons, the hem decorated with silvery lace.

"We have heard, *señor*, of your knowledge of science as well as the arts." Her voice was mellow and warm. "My husband and I would be most pleased to entertain you at our home and to share with you our humble art collection, of which some pieces are the work of the gentleman at your side." She nodded, smiling at Goya, before returning her gaze to Gaspar.

"I am honored, *señora*, to accept your kind invitation."

He watched the couple move away, exchanging greetings with other guests.

"They have a country house outside the city. The Duchess is an intelligent woman and an excellent horsewoman."

Goya's voice drew Gaspar's attention from the departing couple. "Poets and painters are often guests at her table. I have had several commissions from her."

Gaspar smiled at the painter, who brimmed with information about the people whom he had spent considerable time sketching and painting.

The evening had become a swirl of colors and a hum of voices for Gaspar. Hungry as well as fatigued, he noticed a table laden with fruits and cakes in the center of the ballroom, but surrounded by a clog of chattering guests.

No chance of getting through that crowd, he thought. The blur of color and sound continuing, he was relieved when Juan Arias suggested their departure.

"Have you had enough of Spanish society for this evening, my friend?" Saavedra smiled at him.

Moving toward the ballroom door, Juan Arias scanned the room to bid farewell to Campomanes, while Gaspar looked about for Goya, having lost him in the confusing blur.

Almost at the exit, he saw the dark, curly head and piercing eyes pushing through the crowd toward him. The painter raised his hands, each of which held a small, golden cake. Extending one to Juan Arias, he broke the other in half for Gaspar and himself, and the three men stood together munching the confections.

"You managed the crowd, Francisco," Gaspar grinned. He was beginning to think that this slightly-disheveled artist, with the deepset, observant eyes could find his way past any obstacle.

Saying farewell, he promised, on Francisco's insistence, to visit his studio soon.

CHAPTER ELEVEN
At the Artist's Studio

Several weeks filled with work, conferences, reports, and investigations followed the evening at the Campomanes house. A second meeting with Cabarrús proved informative and pleasant, and Gaspar began to enjoy his friendship with the accomplished and intelligent Frenchman turned Spaniard.

He had not forgotten his promise to Goya, and on a fine autumn afternoon with the setting sun bathing Madrid in a warm, yellow glow, Gaspar, a cloak thrown over his jacket against the crisp air, climbed a narrow flight of stairs and knocked at the door of a second-floor landing.

He waited and was considering another rap when Francisco opened the door. The two men beamed with pleasure and grasped hands.

"*Señor* Jovellanos, I am honored to welcome you to my home. Please come in."

A sweeping glance revealed a combination of living area and art studio. Wood-backed canvases of varying sizes leaned against the walls, while a large easel stood near a long double window opened to the waning sunlight. Gaspar saw a small, iron balcony beyond the opening and near the window a table cluttered with jars and brushes. Across the room a smaller table flanked by two chairs held leftovers from a meal. He glanced at the artist and grinned.

"My hat amuses you, Gaspar?" The painter smiled, gesturing to his head, where a crumpled black hat held small flickering candles in its curled brim.

Looks like a squashed birthday cake, Gaspar thought.

"I need the hat to paint when I lose the light from the window," Francisco explained. "It is hard for me to stop, and the night can be very long when I want to work." He removed the hat, extinguished the candles, and placed it on his work table. "But enough of painting for now. Let me offer you some refreshment and then, perhaps, you would care to review my humble efforts."

"With pleasure. *Gracias*." Gaspar took one of the chairs at the table as the painter moved to the door of an adjoining room. Briefly alone, his eyes scanned the canvases and drawings in the room, his interest growing as he looked at the artwork. His attention was diverted by a swish of silk, and he turned to see a woman follow the artist into the room. Gaspar was immediately on his feet.

Francisco spoke gently to the woman, "This is Gaspar Jovellanos, about whom I have spoken. *Señor*, may I present to you my wife, Josefa."

Gaspar bowed, and Josefa curtsied lightly. "It is my pleasure to meet you, *señora*." The woman's quiet, brown eyes met Gaspar's gaze, a slight pink rising in her cheeks. A neatly pinned plait of golden brown hair encircled her head, while small wispy curls fluffed at her forehead. A lace shawl covered the shoulders of her black silk dress.

Unlike the dazzle of the Duquesa d'Alba or the confident independence of the Duquesa de Osuna, Josefa's beauty was quiet, calm, and composed, and Gaspar liked her immediately.

"Please, *señor*, make yourself comfortable." The pink deepened.

Gaspar regained his chair, as Josefa cleared the small clutter from the table and left the room. Francisco sat across from him smiling delightedly as his wife returned with a pot of chocolate, two cups, and sweet rolls on a small tray. Pouring the chocolate, she passed the cups to the men.

"*Gracias, señora.*" Gaspar accepted the cup and pastry offered to him. Josefa, not looking up, nodded slightly. The wisps of hair had been brushed back from her face.

She moved across the room to sit with her sewing basket near the fireplace to listen to the men's conversation and occasionally to steal a glance at Gaspar sitting relaxed, enjoying the warm chocolate and the sketches Francisco was sharing with him.

"As you can see, Gaspar, I have asked Velázquez to be my teacher," the painter explained with a smile.

Gaspar studied the copies Francisco had made of the earlier master's work.

"When looking for a teacher," he replied, "one should always seek quality, and you have chosen the best that Spain can offer. These are, I see, heads and figures after his painting, '*Las Meninas.*'"

Francisco nodded, appreciating Gaspar's knowledge of art and his quick recognition of the masterwork upon which he had based his copies.

"It is a superb effort, perhaps his masterpiece," the artist became effusive, his appreciation of Velázquez and his own passion for art firing him, energizing his speech. Gaspar raised his eyes from the drawings and smiled at Francisco's enthusiasm.

"Notice the placement of the *Infanta* in the composition and her handmaidens around her. See the dog lying to one side," Francisco pointed to each feature of the copies as he spoke, "and Velázquez himself here in the painting. All look out at us, but are they really seeing us?"

Gaspar smiled. "It is the mirror, Francisco, the mirror in the background tells us everything."

"We know that the King and Queen were present," Francisco picked up Gaspar's thought, "watching the *Infanta*, watching the artist work. We know because the mirror tells us so." He paused, "Amazing...amazing."

They sat in silence, musing over the copies and finishing the chocolate.

"May I look at some of your other work, *mi amigo*?" Gaspar asked quietly.

They stood and Francisco shared his sketches for paintings and cartoons for tapestries. On a side table, several charcoal sketches of bulls and the men who face them in the arena caught Gaspar's eye. "I see that you are in favor of this ancient and barbaric ritual," he said, teasing the artist.

"Since boyhood," Francisco answered soberly, his eyes misty and faraway, "I have dreamed of the *Corrida de Toros*." Gaspar grinned and moved away from the drawings.

Finally, they reached the easel beside the window, where Francisco had been adding final brushstrokes, completing a full-length portrait of a hunter holding a long rifle, a large, white dog resting at his feet. The subject, slightly stooped, wore a black tri-cornered hat, a long gray coat over a golden yellow waistcoat, and black boots. He carried a hunter's bag and white gloves, a wide, blue satin sash crossed his chest. Gaspar studied the thin face, long nose, lips turned in a smile, and especially the intelligent, dark eyes looking out at him from the painting.

"King Carlos III," he said quietly. "You have caught him well, Francisco. Under that humble, amiable face lives a brilliant mind. Spain is progressing under his guidance and vision."

"May God grant him a long life," the artist replied.

*   *   *

Days later, alone in the small garden of his Madrid residence as mild autumn air lingered in the city, Gaspar worked at the table, writing reports on economic plans, agricultural reform, and a favored topic, education. He had personal letters to write as well, one to Saavedra, who had moved from the city to his home at Jadraque in nearby Guadalajara province, and another to his brother, Francisco de Paula, at home in Gijón.

Pedro came to attend to him, his footsteps barely audible in the courtyard. *"Más café, señor?"* he asked, prepared to refill Gaspar's cup.

"No, *Gracias*, Pedro. I am finished here for now. I think that I will take a *paseo* to clear my head."

Gaspar enjoyed the late afternoon sunlight of Madrid, and as he walked, his thoughts were of Francisco de Goya and his visit to the artist's studio.

Very gifted, he reflected. *He will one day take his place among the giants of Spanish art.*

His thoughts drifted to the painter's portrait of their beloved King. Gaspar's dreams and plans for progress and reforms had found sympathetic ears in Carlos III. The King shared ideas with those who were endeavoring to raise Spain to the levels of other European nations through reforms and education.

Gaspar's career had flourished during the King's reign. He had worked hard to achieve his goals, quickly earning acceptance in Madrid's most prestigious academies and societies. His opinions were respected and sought in many areas from farming and mining to economics, education, painting, literature, and architecture. A member of the important Economic Society, he had voted in favor of admitting women with full and equal rights.

Surely God would hear Goya's prayer and grant the King a long life and a reign in which Spain would continue to prosper. Unknown to Gaspar, however, the time of King Carlos III was ending, and the news of his death, when it came in 1787, shocked the capital and spread quickly through Spain.

Cabarrús rushed over with the news, and when he was gone, Gaspar sat in his drawing room, deeply saddened, fingering the papers scattered on his desk, his thoughts drifting to Saavedra, wishing he could talk with his friend. In the courtyard a light rain fell through the trees, pattering on the stones and earth below them.

What kind of king will Charles IV be? he wondered. *Will he, like his father, encourage, even allow light to spread through Spain? Will the reformers continue to influence the Corte and the government? And what of the storm gathering in France? Will the violence that I feel will surely come to Paris cross the Pyrenees and threaten Madrid?* He stood and gathered his papers. *We need gradual change and reform with a monarch who cares deeply for his people and guides their progress. Let us hope that Charles IV can fill his father's shoes.* He stood surrounded by his beloved books gazing at the rain.

CHAPTER TWELVE
The Royal Reception

The new King of Spain and his Queen arrived in the capital and moved into the Royal Palace. The city was again vibrantly alive; having buried one monarch, it welcomed the next. News of the royal couple's first gala reception spread rapidly through the ministries. Gaspar was invited to present himself to the new king and to his wife and family.

He smiled, amused, watching Pedro brushing and fussing with his jacket and top hat. He wore a simple, elegant suit, black pants, gray jacket, white stockings and shirt, a cravat tied carefully around his neck. He had allowed Pedro to shave him and neatly brushing back his own hair at the *espejo*, noticed the first tinges of gray.

Helping Gaspar into his jacket, Pedro stepped back to pass a critical eye over his tall, refined master, who, suppressing another smile, struck an elegant, somewhat exaggerated, pose. The pudgy face of the kindly servant lighted with pleasure and satisfaction.

"*Excelente, señor,*" he complimented him. "*Excelente.*"

Downstairs, standing by the fireplace, Gaspar glanced through some papers until the arrival of Francisco de Goya was announced.

Pedro placed a cloak over his shoulders and handed his gloves and hat to him.

"A pleasant evening, *señor*," he nodded.

"*Muchas Gracias, Pedro.*"

In the front driveway, head raised proudly, Francisco sat in a single horse-drawn, open cabriolet. Gaspar had learned of his friend's appointment as court painter and of his recent purchase but had not expected to travel this evening to the Royal Palace in such a sporting carriage.

"Good evening, Francisco." He climbed in beside the artist on the comfortably plush seat. "Very nice," he complimented him, glancing about the vehicle's interior. "Very nice, indeed." Noticing the familiar faraway, misty look in his friend's eyes, he braced himself against the seat.

The artist clucked to the horse, and with a quick slap of the reins, the carriage and its two well-dressed occupants bolted from the drive. As the horse trotted briskly toward the palace, Gaspar managed an air of nonchalance, even as Francisco, exhilarated by his new purchase, drove the horse too quickly, careening the carriage around corners. The night air crisp, the Spanish sky filled with stars, Gaspar's spirits rose in the company of his exuberant friend.

The Royal Palace glistened with candlelight as the cabriolet approached. Entering the drive too quickly, it caught a wheel on the curbing, bounced its gentlemen occupants, and pulled up in a rush to the front portal. A palace groom stepped forward to steady the excited horse while two astonished footmen stood at attention.

Grinning, Gaspar and Francisco alighted from the carriage and entered the palace with other formally-dressed gentlemen amid a swirl and swish of ladies' silks and satins. They proceeded slowly through the crowded corridors toward the throne room and the royal reeception.

Moving into the room, Gaspar stared, not at the royals standing at the far end of the room, but at the high ceiling's immense fresco. Francisco followed his friend's gaze upward to the work of Giovanni Battista Tiepolo and stood with him admiring the swirl of colors, clouds, and figures.

"The Italian was a master of perspective," the artist murmured to Gaspar. "It is called 'Allegory of the Grandeur of the Spanish Monarchy.'"

Gaspar observed that the composition included figures from each of the Spanish provinces as well as from Spain's New World possessions. In the center, figures in bold, dramatic poses symbolized the majesty of Spain's monarchs.

"The figures are perfectly proportioned," Francisco continued, one artist critiquing another, "the colors bold, bright, confidant. The theme blends allegory and reality. Quite remarkable."

"*Buenas Noches, señor Jovellanos.*" A voice at Gaspar's shoulder brought his gaze from the ceiling. He turned and smiled.

"Good evening, *señor* Cabarrús. How is the world of banking this evening?" he asked good-naturedly.

Cabarrús, again dressed in his yellow-gold brocade suit, put his palms together and looking heavenward. Gaspar laughed, and the trio strolled slowly through the chattering press of elegantly dressed guests. As they joined a line that approached the royals from the right and moved slowly in front of the family, they heard a royal crier loudly announce each guest.

Gaspar counted ten family members including the king and queen in the center of the group. He followed Cabarrús and Goya and approaching the first royals, the Prince and Princess of Parma, heard his name called.

"Gaspar Melchor de Jovellanos."

Gaspar nodded to the couple, bowing slightly, his keen gaze meeting the eyes of the prince, a young man dressed in rose-colored silks, a blue and white sash across his chest. His wife, in a gray silk and lace gown, avoided his gaze.

Gaspar saw the chubby face of the *Infante* Antonio Pascual, disinterested and bored. The crowded room grew close and stifling, and Gaspar, resisting an urge to raise his handkerchief and mop his brow, found himself, at last, before the new King and Queen of Spain.

Charles IV in a black satin suit glistening with medals, a red vest, and the distinctive blue and white sash, was tall, heavyset, his pudgy face rosy in the candlelight. He wore a gray wig, curling at his ears.

The king responded to Gaspar's respectful bow with a slight smile. The guests behind him eased him forward until he stood looking into the black eyes of Queen Maria Luisa. She, too, was tall and a bit plump, with black hair piled in curls on a head held regally high and adorned with a jeweled arrow hairpin. She wore a gown of white silk trimmed with black and gold lace. At her sides her children, the *Infanta* Maria Isabel and the *Infante* Francisco de Paula, stood expressionless.

The little royals seem a bit dazed, perhaps bored, Gaspar thought. Nodding and bowing to the queen, he smiled kindly at the children, who did not return his courtesy.

Attempting to move on, the queen's staring, unblinking eyes fixed him in place. Penetrating and cold, her gaze disturbed him, and he was happy when the line pushed him away from her.

He nodded courteously to the remainder of the royals, the aging *Infanta* Maria Josefa, with a pleasant, if somewhat distant smile, the *Infante* Ferdinand, rosy cheeked, standing stiffly in a blue silk suit, and beyond Ferdinand's shoulder, peeking out, the boyish face of the *Infante* Carlos Maria Isidro.

Freed from the line, Gaspar felt somehow deflated, confused, vaguely troubled. The room had grown insufferably warm, and the glittering candles swam before his eyes. Cabarrús had vanished, swallowed by the crowd. Francisco, at his side, turned him toward the exit and fresh air.

A few steps from the corridor, a man's loud laughter stopped him, the bold sound startling in the dignified setting. Gaspar turned to see a large, ample figure sitting casually reclined against a side wall. The man, a sword at his side, wore a black, short jacket with red velvet facing, beige pants, and boots to his knees. His round, ruddy, animated face exuded confidence. He laughed heartily again.

A dark-haired woman sat at his side, her pale skin luminous around black eyes and full, red lips. A black and gold short jacket covered the top of a white silk gown tied lightly at the waist by a pink sash.

The man spoke to her, and in response she threw back her head, mouth opened wide, and exploded in laughter. Gaspar started again, astonished at the woman's behavior.

"He is Emmanuel Godoy, a Royal Guardsman," Francisco said, smiling at his friend's bewildered face, "He is a considerable favorite of the queen. Although young, he is a rising star in the royal constellation and will, no doubt, soon be named Prime Minister."

"And the woman?" Gaspar asked

"She is Pepita Tudó, a friend of the gentleman."

Gaspar exhaled slowly and turning from the couple was astonished to find from a distance the dark, staring eyes of the queen still fixed on him. His unease increasing, he was relieved finally to reach the corridor.

"Well, my dear Gaspar, how does it feel to have gone from the sublime to the ridiculous in one evening?" Goya chuckled, breathing cool air at last. "From the majestic Tiepolo to the royal family and Godoy." He glanced at his elegant friend, his eyes twinkling mischievously. In response, Gaspar managed something between a slight grin and a painful grimace.

Regaining their hats and cloaks, they waited outside for Francisco's horse and cabriolet.

"He lacks the ability of Charles III," Francisco said quietly, when they were seated in the carriage, waiting for the traffic to clear and allow passage onto the road, "but I hear that his intentions are good."

"He will need to surround himself with good and wise advisors, not the false flatterers and self-seekers that all too often surround the powerful," Gaspar replied thoughtfully. The palace traffic moved slowly forward.

"What of the queen?" he asked, the black eyes still troubling him. "I do not think that I made a good impression on her."

Francisco snorted and turned to his friend. "I would not worry about that," he said. "I have much to tell you about life at the court."

Gaspar would have to wait for details, because Francisco's carriage had cleared the palace grounds and on the open road again, encouraged by its driver, the horse resumed its brisk pace.

Returning home, braced securely on the cabriolet's seat, Gaspar chuckled at the wild glow in his companion's eyes. Standing at last in his driveway, he bade good night to his adventurous friend. "Francisco, I have enjoyed the ride enormously, but please take care driving home."

The artist answered with a grin, a lift of his eyebrows, and a sharp flick of the whip. The horse bolted forward, and the cabriolet, turning too quickly into the street, caught part of the rock curbing. Tilting for a long, precarious moment, it righted itself with a jolting thud. Francisco disappeared down the dark street in a clatter of hooves.

CHAPTER THIRTEEN
On the Road Again

Gaspar spent the following days buried in work, and as the royal reception receded to a distant memory, his natural good spirits revived. One morning, a message, a commission arrived from the royal court ordering him to travel west to the university city of Salamanca to review and prepare a report on the faculty and programs of the College of Calatrava. Afterwards, he would continue north to examine and report on carbon mining in Asturias. Upon the completion of these assignments, he would return to Madrid.

Delighted to visit his literary friends in Salamanca with whom he had corresponded since his days in Seville, Gaspar was happy, also, to return to his beloved Asturias. He gave word to Pedro to prepare for his trip and to ready Robles.

The following morning, he found Francisco de Goya alone in his upstairs studio. Accepting the coffee cup offered to him, he glanced about the intriguing room. There were new sketches and canvases. One, in particular, caught his eye, a dark-haired woman reclining on a sofa.

Francisco followed his friend's gaze and awaited his comments.

"Take care, *amigo*, you may have to wear the *coroza* for this one," Gaspar chuckled, approaching the painting.

"I do not believe that the Office of the Inquisition favors portraits of women without clothing. Perhaps it is for your personal collection?"

"Godoy commissioned it," Francisco replied easily, unaffected by Gaspar's teasing. "It is for his apartment, along with this one."

He reached behind the canvas and raised another, still in the sketching stage, of the same woman on the sofa. It was a replica of the first painting, except that the woman in the sketch was clothed.

"The prime minister intends to hang the first painting over his fireplace with this second one over it," Francisco explained, "whenever he has guests."

Gaspar smiled, slowly shaking his head.

They sat at the small table to drink their coffee and chat. Relaxing, Gaspar leaned an elbow on the table and rested his head on his hand, as he gazed about the studio. From the corner of an eye, he noted that Francisco, holding a piece of charcoal and a tablet, glanced at him as he sketched. Inwardly pleased, he pretended to be unaware of the artist's efforts to capture his likeness and told him of his commission to Salamanca.

"I will be away a fortnight or so," he concluded, before rising to leave. "And Francisco," he said, eyes twinkling, "if you are called to wear the *coroza* before the Inquisitors for that dark-haired beauty you have created, perhaps you could mention your trip to Italy. Italian artists are highly respected in Spain. Yes, mention their influence on you. It might save you." With a grin, he tapped his hat and left his friend.

*　*　*

The road from Madrid to Salamanca led northwest across the Meseta. Gaspar left the dozing capital in the early morning and smiling at his horse's eager energy, let Robles canter.

"The open road again, my boy." He patted the animal, drawing rein to slow his pace. "We must save our energy, Robles. It is a long way to Salamanca."

Reaching an inn by nightfall, Gaspar settled Robles in the adjoining stable before entering the lodging. The innkeeper, quick to notice a gentleman's demeanor, rushed to him and bowed.

"*Señor*, we are honored by your presence in our humble inn. Will it please you to dine with us this evening?"

Weary from his ride and wanting to sleep, Gaspar thanked the man, asking only for a bed and some bread and cheese.

Holding a candle aloft, he surveyed his room, noted the cobwebs and unswept floor, the curtainless windows opaque with grime, a wooden chair, and a bulging, gray lump of mattress on a rough, wooden bed. Exhausted, he pulled off his coat and boots and lay down. Sighing deeply, he closed his eyes. The candle, placed on the chair, flickered low in its dish.

Slap! He swatted something on his leg. "Ay!" He scratched his shoulder. On his feet in a flash, Gaspar held the dying flame over the bed and grimaced.

"*Chinches!*"

The mattress was full of bedbugs.

"Ay!" Gaspar scratched his leg. "*Pulgas!*" he said in disgust. "Ay, yi, yi! This flea holds on like a bulldog."

Moments later, Robles nickered a soft welcome to his master.

"Good Evening, my friend," Gaspar said, reaching for the horse's blanket, folded neatly beside the stall. "I trust you do not mind sharing your quarters this evening. I will be more comfortable here than in the inn."

Wrapping the blanket about him, he settled down in the straw next to the horse's stall and sighing again, closed his eyes. The fine, gray head reached down over the stall gate, the soft muzzle brushing the shoulder of the gentleman asleep on the floor.

CHAPTER FOURTEEN
A Dangerous Decision

Gaspar and Robles approached Salamanca after a long day's ride and by late evening, crossed the Rio Tormes into the slumbering city.

"This bridge, Robles," Gaspar explained, continuing his horse's education, "was built by the Romans, who lived here long ago. They were outstanding engineers and knew how to build structures that would endure."

The next morning, he began his review of the College of Calatrava and after several days of intense work examining courses of study with the faculty, completed his commission.

Needing only to add finishing touches to his written report, Gaspar enjoyed a *paseo* along Salamanca's narrow, winding streets and arrived at noon in the Plaza Mayor, the main square in the city center. He strolled under its covered colonnade admiring the ornate facades of the golden-yellow buildings framing the plaza.

From a table in a shaded corner, he gazed at the sunlit square, while a server brought him a stew of vegetables and beans, a large chunk of crusty bread, and a glass of red wine.

Spreading a *servilleta* across his lap and suddenly aware of his hunger, Gaspar lifted his fork and was about to dig into the meal, when a voice close on his right startled him.

"Gaspar, a thousand pardons, but I learned this morning of your arrival."

Surprised by the familiarity of the greeting, Gaspar rose to face a small, stout, dark-haired man with a round, flat, amiable face. A companion, taller and quietly serious, stood behind him. Both wore the clothing of gentlemen.

Gaspar stared at the shorter man. "Bermudo?" he asked, incredulously.

"*Sí*, Gaspar, it is I."

"We are a long way from Gijón," Gaspar smiled with delight at the sight of his boyhood friend, Juan Ceán Bermúdez. "What brings you to Salamanca?"

"I am on my way to Seville," the man responded eagerly, "I have been commissioned to begin a catalog of Spanish artwork. I would appreciate your input, Gaspar, if it would please you."

"Bermudo, I will be happy to help you in any way that I can." Gaspar glanced at the man standing behind him.

"Forgive me, Gaspar," the younger man said quickly, "may I present to you, Juan Antonio Meléndez Valdés. I believe that you are acquainted through correspondence."

Gaspar smiled again, extending his hand to the poet. Learning of him from Olavide long ago in Seville, he had exchanged letters with the writer and others of the literary group in Salamanca.

"*Señor* Meléndez, I am honored. Will you, gentlemen, please join me for lunch?"

The three settled down happily to food, wine, and conversation.

"*Señor* Jovino," Meléndez began, using Gaspar's pen name, "I very much appreciate your letters. Your comments on my work and suggestions for my poetic efforts have been very valuable to me." He dipped a crust of bread into his wine to soften it.

Gaspar nodded his acceptance of the compliment. "I enjoy reading your poetry very much," he responded in kind. "It is the need for educational reform, however, that brings me to Salamanca."

With that, the three men lapsed into a discussion of Gaspar's ideas for moving Spain forward into the modern era.

"We must educate all levels of society," Gaspar explained, "Education must be for everyone." They engaged in lively conversation, and as always, Gaspar reveled in the exchange of ideas. The server brought slices of fried pastry to dip into cups of thick, hot chocolate.

At this pleasant moment, however, a messenger from the College approached the table and—bowing to the men—handed a letter to Meléndez. He read it quickly, before passing it to Gaspar. "This may interest you."

Reading the letter, Gaspar's face grew serious. "Cabarrús has been arrested and imprisoned in Madrid on charges of financial misdealings in his banking work. How can this be possible?"

"He may be worrisome to the powerful in Madrid," Bermudo sought to explain, "because he is from France."

"The turmoil in Paris, the revolution, is troubling to all of Europe's monarchs," Meléndez continued, "and I am sure that you know how easily lies and innuendo can spread."

Gaspar nodded thoughtfully. He was aware that snakes could lie unseen in the grass. "His ideas may seem threatening to some," he mused. "The thought of change can frighten people."

He stood suddenly, the two men following him to their feet. Gaspar had made up his mind and knew what he had to do.

"*Señor* Meléndez, it has been a pleasure to meet you. Bermudo, I will write to you in Seville. I am sorry to end our meeting so abruptly, but I must return to Madrid at once."

Bermudo's face grew pale. "Gaspar, you have not completed your assignment," he protested, "and you cannot return until you do."

"I have finished my work here," Gaspar replied calmly, "and as for visiting the mines in Asturias, I will do so after a brief return to Madrid."

Deeply worried, Bermudo continued his attempts to dissuade Gaspar from leaving. "Consider the risk you are taking in disobeying orders and returning without permission, not to mention the dangers of aligning yourself with someone accused of crimes."

Gaspar grinned at his boyhood friend, "I remember a time long ago, Bermudo, when you wanted me to do something wrong."

"I'm serious, Gaspar."

Gaspar looked at the man a moment, his eyes warm with affection and appreciation for his concern. "Bermudo, he is my friend. I cannot let him face these charges alone."

The following day, Robles, carrying his thoughtful master, retraced his hoofprints back toward the capital, back to the intrigue and gossip of the court, to the jealousies, fears, and untruths that can lie in the grass, waiting.

CHAPTER FIFTEEN
Uprooted

A rriving in Madrid at nightfall, Gaspar stabled Robles and declining gratefully Pedro's offer of a meal, walked under a moonless sky to the Campomanes house.

He is influential and no doubt will support my defense of Cabarrús and help win his release from prison, he reasoned, approaching the dwelling and noting with satisfaction that candles burned in several of its windows. A servant accepted his hat and cloak in the entrance hallway.

"Gaspar Jovellanos to see *el señor* Campomanes, *por favor.*"

Pacing impatiently, Gaspar contemplated the gilt-framed mirrors and paintings in the room. Glancing down the hall after the servant, he frowned, folded his arms, and continued to walk. Bewildered by the delay, he looked again down the hall. At last, the servant emerged from a room far down on the left and head down, hurried toward the foyer.

"I am sorry, *señor*," he said, not looking up. "*El señor* Campomanes regrets that he is unable to see you tonight."

Gaspar started, amazed, feeling his face go warm. *Surely he knows why I am here,* he thought numbly, dazed by the unexpected rejection.

The servant, avoiding his eyes, returned his cloak and hat. Suddenly, he was on the street, the door shut quickly and firmly behind him.

Gaspar strode through the dark night, his face flushed from the humiliation and shock of being turned away by the public prosecutor. *Why will he not help a friend?* he thought. *Why are people afraid to stand up in defense of what they know to be right? Surely Cabarrús is innocent.* Thoroughly disgusted with Campomanes, Gaspar knew that the episode would sever their connection.

Irritated, he pressed on, trusting his feet to find their way home, while his mind churned. He needed another strategy to help Cabarrús.

Pedro, dozing in a chair in the foyer, leaped up as Gaspar entered the house. Shocked by the turbulence he read in his master's face, he walked quickly to him, asking if he could do or get anything for him.

Consumed by angry thoughts and starting at the interruption, Gaspar turned sharply to face the little man. The kindly, concerned eyes sobered him, and staring at Pedro, he forced a smile.

"*Gracias*, Pedro," he said quietly, "I do not think that I could eat anything this evening. I will go to bed now. *Buenas Noches.*"

Gaspar slept fitfully, his inner turmoil robbing him of much needed rest. In the morning Pedro brought a tray with coffee, bread, and honey. Sensing that his master intended to go hungry, the kindly servant refused to leave until Gaspar ate something.

Toward midmorning a messenger arrived. Pedro brought the letter to Gaspar in the drawing room. A royal missive, reading it, his face clouded, and when he had finished, he stared at the paper for a long time.

Pedro stood watching uneasily, unsettled by the change in the pleasant, good-natured man. He had never seen him upset or angry.

At last, Gaspar looked up from the letter. "I will be leaving Madrid again, Pedro," he began in a quiet, steady voice, "this time for a while. I will need you to pack all of my belongings, clothing, books, everything, and send them to my family's house in Gijón. When you have done that, you will return to the home of Juan Arias de Saavedra in Jadraque." He paused, looking quietly at the little man. "We must part company, Pedro. I am going home to Asturias."

With that, Gaspar walked through the double doors into the courtyard. Pedro waited a few moments to regain his composure before going quickly to begin the packing.

Gaspar knew that the letter from the Royal Court was a response to his return to Madrid. Failing to complete his commission, he was now officially relieved of his duties in the ministry and assigned to an indefinite stay in Asturias during which he would review the mines and agriculture of his native region.

He sensed there was more to the story of his exile from the capital. He realized that his display of independence on behalf of an imprisoned friend had come at a difficult time and that his action had irritated those in power, who felt threatened by the revolution and violence in neighboring France.

He knew, as well, that there were those near the king, perhaps the queen herself, who would be pleased at his dismissal and take satisfaction in his fall from authority and influence. No matter how noble his goals, he knew that some feared and resented him on a personal level because of his talents and ability. Thus, relieved of his duties, he was being sent home indefinitely from Madrid.

In two days, ready to leave, he said farewell to Pedro and penned an explanation to Goya, who had gone south to Cadiz to complete a painting commission.

In the front drive Pedro waited with a letter delivered by a servant of Campomanes. The scrawled message to Gaspar was brief:

Señor Jovellanos,

I have no desire to be a hero, and even if I did, I would not know how.

Gaspar crumpled the paper and cast it to the ground.

*   *   *

As Robles walked slowly from the Madrid residence, Gaspar contemplated his departure from the city. Feeling somewhat humiliated and disgraced by his dismissal, he considered turning Robles toward a less-traveled street away from the eyes of anyone who might be enjoying his fall from power. Having reached the main avenue, however, the horse, aware of the crowd and sensing an available audience, launched without direction into its neck-arched, prancing step.

"Robles, humility does not seem to be one of your virtues," Gaspar chuckled, patting the animal's neck. "Well, my boy, let us show the *Madrileños* how members of the Jovellanos family depart from a city. It will take more than exile to defeat us."

His relaxed, confident air returning, Gaspar straightened in the saddle and allowed the spirited Robles to proceed along the road in his fine Andalusian gait.

Down the long avenue of poplars, past rose bushes, fountains, and the Royal Palace, the magnificent horse and his elegant rider passed in full view of Spanish society. At the edge of the city, where the flat, dry roads began their meander over the Meseta, Gaspar finally drew rein.

"Well done, Robles. Thank you for reminding me that it is always better to keep one's chin up."

The horse, eager for the open road, snorted impatiently. Smiling, Gaspar turned into the road leading northwest, toward the mountains, the trees, and the sea, toward Asturias. Starting at a trot, Gaspar soon loosened the reins and let Robles run.

CHAPTER SIXTEEN
Francisco de Paula

Robles picked his way over the rocky Asturian terrain. After the heat of the Meseta, the crisp, cool air of the highlands and the green, the glorious green, welcomed and refreshed the homeward bound Gaspar, buoying his spirits. There were trees everywhere, poplars, chestnuts, elms, and oaks, and he smiled with pleasure at the sight of them, .

"Look there, Robles," he said, stopping the horse at the rocky summit of a hill. "There is el Mar Cantábrico. See how blue it is, so marvelously blue against all the green of our land."

They continued northward toward the patches of cultivated earth near the coastline following the road into Gijón toward the plaza and the house of the Jovellanos family.

Gaspar returned to his beloved city on a day warm with late summer sunshine. At midday, Gijón was hushed, dozing. The breeze carried the scent of saltwater to him, and he saw the bell tower of his church and beyond, the wharf at water's edge. Riding calmly into the city, his heart leaped at the sight of a familiar figure.

Standing in the doorway of the front portico of the Jovellanos home, his brother, Francisco de Paula, a hand over his eyes, looked toward an approaching horse and rider. Suddenly, he started and moved quickly into the square.

Gaspar dismounted and the brothers embraced.

"Welcome home, Gaspar," Francisco de Paula said, his handsome face flushed with happiness and tears welling in his dark eyes. "It has been too long."

A young stable boy approached and reaching for Robles's rein, bowed to Gaspar. *"Buenos días, señor Jovellanos. I am Felipe."*

Gaspar gave a few words of instruction, before allowing the boy to lead the animal toward the stable and patting Robles as he passed.

"I see you have brought a part of Andalusia home with you to Asturias," Francisco de Paula said admiringly. *"Es magnífico."*

The house was much as Gaspar had remembered it only quieter since the passing of his parents. He stood for a moment watching rays of sunlight slanting through the dwelling's tall windows.

"The house is empty, Gaspar," Francisco de Paula explained. "My wife, Gertrudis, is away visiting her family. Come, I have prepared rooms for you." He led his brother to a bedroom with an adjoining library. "The servants will look after our needs. Rest now, and we will have something to eat shortly." He turned back in the doorway. "I am happy to have you home, *mi hermano.*"

*   *   *

Settling quickly into a routine, Gaspar spent much of his time with Robles, wandering the countryside, observing land usage, irrigation systems, and carbon mines. He noted how coal was shipped along waterways and examined the conditions of roads. Sometimes, on longer excursions, he visited churches to view their architectural styles and artwork. Always, he recorded his observations, thoughts, and suggestions for improvements in notebooks for later use in written reports.

At home, he took daily walks, usually to the wharf and along the shoreline, often in the company of his brother. In the afternoon, he welcomed visitors, friends, and neighbors, to whom the Jovellanos door had always been open, and who now came to chat with him, to share their problems, and to seek his counsel.

Evenings were spent by the fireplace, reading books and newspapers, including those written in French and English. His days full and pleasant; Gaspar soon realized that although he missed his former life in Madrid, he was enjoying exile.

One afternoon, during a *paseo* with Francisco de Paula along the windswept shoreline, Gaspar shared his dream of establishing a school in Gijón, the Royal Asturian Institute of Navigation and Mineralogy, dedicated to his ideas for educational reform. The students, thirteen years and older, having completed elementary education, would continue their studies in math, science, economics, and the humanities and learn useful skills. They would study in their native tongue and learn other languages in a nurturing, respectful environment.

"Francisco, the Institute will have books from many countries, and I will find the best teachers. I will seek contributions to help with expenses." Gaspar's mind was alive with ideas for his new venture. "I plan also to open a free elementary school for poor boys and have written to our sister, Josefa. She has agreed to do the same for girls in her village." He grinned happily, "Education is for everyone."

Francisco de Paula, intrigued by and smiling at his brother's enthusiasm, said, "I will support you in everything you do, Gaspar. Tell me how I can help you."

"You can teach at the Institute, Francisco," Gaspar said, gratefully, "You are well educated in nautical sciences. I, too, will teach some classes, probably languages."

Francisco de Paula nodded. "And I will donate one of the buildings I own on the plaza to house the Institute."

Gaspar smiled with pleasure at his brother's generosity.

CHAPTER SEVENTEEN
"Education is for Everyone!"

The school, established in an elegant old structure on the square not far from the Jovellanos house, was soon open and thriving with an eager group of young scholars.

His active mind engaged in diverse endeavors, Gaspar's days in Gijón, far from the intrigues of court life, continued to pass happily. The welfare of his country and its people remaining his first concern in all of his efforts, he taught French and English classes at the Institute each week, continued his explorations in the countryside, and began a detailed report on agricultural reform.

He kept a personal diary, adding to it daily seated by the fireplace in his room. Each day, he looked forward to the mail delivery and eagerly read the correspondence from friends, who provided him with news of life and events beyond Asturias.

One afternoon, having returned from an overnight excursion in the countryside, he took the previous day's mail to the small garden patio at the rear of the house. In the shade of an apple tree, he read his letters, one from Saavedra telling of Pedro's safe return, another from Meléndez with a new poem for his appraisal, and one from Ceán Bermúdez in Seville sharing thoughts on Murillo.

When he had read all of the letters, Gaspar walked into the garden beyond the patio's wooden gate. Idling along the well-tended rows of vegetables and herbs and enjoying the sun's warmth, he glanced toward the stable.

Robles stood calmly in a small corral, tethered to a railing in the weathered fence around the enclosure. The silvery gray tail flicked, now and then, over his side and back. His deep gray coat glistened in the sun.

Gaspar watched Felipe raise a dripping sponge from a bucket to the horse's side and down a foreleg, washing away the grime and dust from miles of travel. Gaspar, pleased to see Robles relaxed and agreeable under the young boy's care, admired Felipe's confidence with the large animal, as well as his obvious gentleness.

Rubbing Robles with drying cloths, the boy finished his task by grooming the horse's back and sides, while Robles shivered and shrugged under the brush. When he had finished, Felipe untied the horse, allowing him to nose about in the corral's grass, while he returned to the stable.

Gaspar walked to the corral.

Robles, looking up from his grazing, nickered as his master approached.

"Do not let me disturb you. I have come to see Felipe," Gaspar grinned, patting the animal.

At the sound of his name, the boy dropped the hay he was carrying and walked calmly from the stable. Bowing slightly, his young face serious, he stood silently before Gaspar.

Thin and tall for his thirteen years, his unbrushed blond hair was flecked with dust and hay, and a trace of ribs under bronzed skin peaked from a white, billowy cotton shirt, unbuttoned at the neck. Knowing that the boy took his meals in the Jovellanos kitchen, Gaspar surmised that the thinness resulted from rapid growth rather than a poor diet.

"Felipe, I wanted to thank you for the excellent care you are giving to Robles," Gaspar said kindly. "He is a very strong horse and can be a challenge to handle. He seems, however, quite happy in your hands."

The boy smiled, his deep blue eyes meeting Gaspar's gaze.

"Do you go to school, Felipe?"

"I have finished my first letters, *señor*," the boy responded. "Now, I am happy to work for my living." He lowered his eyes. Gaspar said nothing further and walked back to the house in deep thought.

At the front door, he met Francisco de Paula returning with the day's *correo*. There were several letters for Gaspar and a news gazette from London.

The brothers walked into the kitchen, mail in hand, and sat at the wooden table. Late afternoon sunlight streamed through a window. Looking out to the stable yard, Gaspar watched Felipe patting and stroking Robles.

"He has an easy way with the animal," Francisco de Paula observed, "and is developing a strong attachment to it, I believe."

"He should be in school," Gaspar said quietly. "He deserves the opportunity to be educated." He looked toward the adjoining pantry, where Felipe's mother, Clothilde, quietly prepared the evening meal. Entering the room, she placed cups of hot coffee before the men.

"*Gracias, señora*," Francisco de Paula said. A pleasant faced, light-haired woman with her son's blue eyes and thinness, she did not look at the men, but bowing slightly, moved away.

"*Señora, perdón*," Gaspar spoke suddenly.

Francisco de Paula, startled, his eyes widening, looked at his brother curiously. Felipe's mother turned back, blushing deeply.

"*Sí, señor?*" She said questioningly, as Gaspar rose.

"*Señora*, my brother tells me that you and your family have been faithful and caring members of our household for many years." He paused as the woman nodded nervously. "Your son is a good worker and an excellent groom." He paused again, searching for the right words. "*Señora*, I am very grateful for the care he gives to my horse."

"He loves horses, *señor*," the woman responded softly, "and Robles is very special."

Gaspar's kind smile brought another blush. He decided to state his point directly.

"*Señora*, I would like Felipe to enroll and be educated in the Asturian Institute. I would like him to study mathematics, science, economics, and to read poetry and drama," his words tumbled forth, "and to learn languages," he added, then stopped, aware that the woman was staring at him incredulously.

"*Señor, perdoneme, por favor.*" She was trembling. "We are not wealthy. My husband farms on your family's estate. I am your housekeeper, my son your groom. We cannot..."

Gaspar interrupted her. "I will accept the work that Felipe does, the personal care that he shows to Robles in exchange for whatever he may need. I would like him to begin at once."

Dismayed, Gaspar stopped speaking. Large tears had welled in the woman's eyes and spilled over her cheeks. Horrified over the affect of his words, he moved forward, hand extended to console her, but Clothilde, stepping back quickly, raised her hands to stop him.

"*Señor* Jovellanos," she said slowly, struggling to keep her voice from breaking, "my family and I are honored to work in your family's household. We have always been treated with respect and kindness." She took a deep breath.

"You offer to my son a great gift. Schooling is for the rich, for the noble. Felipe is a good boy, my only child." Her voice broke. "My family and I will be forever in your debt." Tears flowed again. This time, she allowed Gaspar to take her hand and press it.

"*Señora*," he spoke softly, kindly, "education is for everyone."

Francisco de Paula, smiling broadly, was on his feet. "My brother and I will find some clothing for Felipe. He can begin his classes this week."

Gaspar, turning to leave, paused, a thoughtful furrow creasing his brow. "I hope that Felipe will share our enthusiasm and approve of our plans."

A smile radiating through the tears on Clothilde's face was Gaspar's answer.

CHAPTER EIGHTEEN
Shaking Trees

L eaving his mail unopened by the fireplace, Gaspar walked with his brother along the coast. The waves crashed against rocks, spraying mist high into the air.

Gaspar and Francisco de Paula, cloaks billowing in the breeze, picked their way along a winding, pebbly path, while the setting sun glazed the terrain before them.

They sat awhile on rocks overlooking the sea. Gaspar gazed, squinting, at the sparkling water, while Francisco studied his brother's face thoughtfully.

"You are kind to women," he said quietly, "and they obviously like you. Why have you not married?"

Gaspar continued to watch the water. Only his brother could ask such a personal question of him. He waited, half expecting the scent of sweet jasmine and the soft splash of a fountain. This time, however, the brisk breeze ruffling his hair, the crash of surf below him, and the salty sea spray on his face blocked memories. He breathed deeply, exhaling slowly.

"Marriage is not for me," he said quietly, not looking at Francisco de Paula, who continued to gaze at him.

"You work too much," his brother said. Gaspar glanced at him, grinning, and looked back to the sea.

"How are the reports progressing?" Francisco de Paula persisted, following his brother's gaze out to the water.

"I am writing on reforming farming methods and land usage, and I hope that the king will read my report," Gaspar replied. "Charles IV is surrounded by people who flatter instead of guide him, who care not about the country or its people but only of their own positions and personal profit."

"Reform is not often a welcome topic to those in control of power and wealth," Francisco observed. "Be careful, *mi hermano*, when you shake a tree, not all of the apples will be happy."

Gaspar smiled at his brother's metaphor. "Charles III welcomed change, encouraged reform."

"Charles III did not have the echo of the guillotine in his ears, Gaspar. The French thinkers have challenged the power of monarchs and are upsetting the social order. It cannot be pleasant for our king to have a Reign of Terror occurring so dangerously close in France and to know that the guillotine has claimed his cousin, Louis XVI, as well as the queen, Marie Antoinette."

Gaspar frowned, watching a wave crash against the shore. "Violence and revolution are not the means to achieve the reforms that are needed in agriculture, education, and economics. Change must occur gradually, not by a violent overthrow of a monarch."

He brought his gaze back to his brother. "Too much land is owned by nobles and clergy and lays idle, uncultivated, Francisco, and too many people do as little as possible in their positions, while living very well off the labors of others."

Francisco de Paula stared at his brother's intense, intelligent eyes, before responding slowly, thoughtfully, "Gaspar, such ideas will frighten some and irritate many and will earn enemies for you. Some may envy your abilities, others resent you as a threat to their positions. Be on your guard. People do not relinquish power or wealth easily. Neither do they change old habits readily. Be careful, *mi hermano*, we live in restless, dangerous times."

Gaspar, seeing the concern in his brother's dark eyes, felt a rush of love and gratitude for him. He looked back at the wind-whipped sea.

"I can fight them in the light, Francisco, but so much of what they do is in the dark."

*   *   *

The fire on the hearth crackled brightly as Gaspar, seated in his armchair, pulled and kicked off his boots. He stretched his legs toward the fire, warming his feet, and unfastened the top buttons of his shirt, before turning to pick up his mail.

Letters from Madrid, one from Cabarrús, free at last and hoping for Gaspar's return to the Capital, one from his sister, Benita, describing her daily routine, which he read with pleasure, and finally, with a surge of happiness, a letter from Goya.

Francisco de Paula, entering the room, saw his brother's smile and settled relaxedly in a chair, arms crossed over his chest, feet before the fire. He sighed contentedly and glanced at Gaspar in time to see the happiness melt from his face.

"What is it, *mi hermano*? What has happened?"

Gaspar lowered the letter slowly to his lap and looked at his brother with troubled eyes. "Francisco de Goya has written to me. It seems that he has been quite ill." He paused, fingering the letter.

"What has happened to him?" Francisco de Paula prodded.

"He had gone south to Cadiz, to visit a friend, Sebastian Martinez, and to complete a portrait commission. Shortly after finishing the painting, he began to have very bad headaches, ringing in his ears, dizziness." Gaspar's voice was low and serious. "He stayed with Martinez until he appeared to be improving, but just when things seemed to be going well, he relapsed. In his words, it was terrible, worse than before, with pounding and ringing, dizziness, and fever."

He gazed at the fire. "He has recovered somewhat, but is still very weak."

Francisco de Paula waited in silence. Gaspar looked at his brother.

"Goya is deaf, Francisco, completely and utterly deaf."

CHAPTER NINETEEN
Courage!

Chattering students crammed the hall of the Institute, as Gaspar, weaving and dodging, endeavored to make his way to the library. A pair of staring, blue eyes caught his attention. Nodding to Felipe, Gaspar noticed that the hay and dust were gone from his fine, pale hair. Books tucked under an arm, the boy moved off down the hall in the company of two schoolmates.

Reaching the *biblioteca* at last, Gaspar greeted the librarian. "Good morning, Juan. Have you been able to locate the book I requested?"

"*Sí*, it is right here." He handed a small volume to Gaspar.

"*Muchas gracias*, Juan."

"*De nada*, Gaspar."

*   *   *

The following day, Gaspar returned from the Institute to find mail awaiting him. Sinking into his chair before the hearth, he picked up a letter and started at the Royal Seal.

What is this? he wondered, quickly opening the missive. Gaspar stared incredulously at the handwriting. Godoy, the Prime Minister, was requesting, on behalf of the King, his thoughts and opinions regarding the Office of the Inquisition! *Is this my chance at last to return to my work in Madrid? Is my exile ending?* he thought eagerly.

His mind flush with ideas, he set to work at once, his pen pouring forth his thoughts. Gaspar argued not for the reform of the Inquisition, but for its extinction. Pointing out the Office's many injustices, he included his countrymen's fear, the unjust power it exerted over their lives and thoughts, the repression of books, the disgrace of Spain in the eyes of other European countries, but especially its abuses against the Church.

Despite intense emotions regarding the subject, he managed to maintain his elegantly clear writing style, even as he poured his soul into the report. To him, the Inquisition was a distortion of his sacred faith and the message of the Gospels, and it had to end.

He worked feverishly, and when he was satisfied with the completed report, dispatched it to Godoy to bring to the attention of the King, and sent his recently completed agrarian essay, in which he advised reforms in the ownership and usage of Spanish land to the prestigious Economic Society in Madrid.

*   *   *

In the garden, the late-afternoon sun warming his back, Gaspar sat with his new book opened on his lap. Glancing from the book to his hands, he wiggled his fingers into different positions.

He did not see Felipe approach. The boy, observing Gaspar in the garden, had stopped his chores to watch him. Fascinated and overwhelmed by curiosity, he approached slowly, quietly.

Looking up, Gaspar smiled at the boy's incredulous stare. "Come here, Felipe, sit down," he said warmly, still grinning.

"Are you all right, *señor*?" The boy asked hesitantly, his concern genuine. "Is your hand all right?"

Gaspar laughed. "Look, Felipe," he used his hand to form shapes. "C-D-F. I am learning another language."

The boy looked carefully at the book and began to form letters with Gaspar.

"Why do you want to learn this new language, *señor*?"

Gaspar paused to look at him. "I have a very good friend, Felipe, whose conversation I miss very much. When I see him again, I want to be able to talk with him."

"*Es sordo, señor*?" the boy asked quietly.

"Yes, he is deaf." Gaspar looked out over the sun-drenched garden. "It is difficult, Felipe, but the human heart is strong and resilient and very often can find a way around an obstacle."

In the sunny patio of the Jovellanos home, practicing a new language with his young student, Gaspar did not know how soon his own heart would be tested.

* * *

Francisco de Goya stood in his darkened second-floor studio. Long windows open to the balcony, he gazed in silence, eyes fixed on the night sky. A breeze stirred Josefa's curtains and caressed his face.

He had returned to Madrid and was working again, despite those who had thought his career would end.

"His deafness will destroy him."

"He will never again pick up a brush."

"The loss, the terrible loss will stifle his talent."

Despite the predictions, he was painting again, perhaps with increased intensity and focus and, with many commissions, was growing comfortably wealthy. He missed his friends, scattered in exile. He missed Jovellanos. *When will we meet again?* he wondered.

*   *   *

Francisco de Paula sank into his chair before the fire, flushed from his brisk walk across the square and brushing October raindrops from his sleeves. He passed a letter to his brother.

"This may interest you," he said nonchalantly.

Gaspar glanced at the letter, noticed the royal seal, and opened it. He read quickly, a worried furrow forming between his eyes.

"Bad news?" his brother inquired.

"Strange news," Gaspar answered, looking at the letter before him. "It seems that I have been appointed Amabassador to Russia."

Francisco de Paula started and turned to his brother. Seeing his shocked expression, Gaspar managed a small smile.

"The letter is from Godoy," he explained. "It is a strange assignment for me, since my background and experience have little to do with diplomacy and foreign negotiations."

"What will you do?" Francisco asked.

"I will write to Godoy, thank him for the assignment and argue that I am unsuited for it given my age, my inexperience in political negotiations, my preference for a tranquil life."

"It is definitely not an ideal position for you," his brother concurred.

"It is not," Gaspar agreed, "but it would seem so to anyone who wanted me far away from Spain. Very possibly, this assignment is a reaction to the reports I sent to Madrid."

Francisco de Paula, his brow furrowed, stared at his brother. "Gaspar, your talent, the respect you enjoy from our countrymen, and the goals you pursue for their benefit frighten and irritate many people. Please think carefully before you respond to Godoy."

Gaspar smiled gratefully at his brother's concern. "I am happy in Asturias and have no desire to give up the tranquility I enjoy here."

Despite the calm demeanor he maintained before his brother, Gaspar spent a restless night, tossing and turning, his mind thick with thoughts of a faraway Russian commission. Displeased with the assignment, he arose before dawn and seated at his writing desk, composed an argument against it in his refined, respectful prose.

Days passed with correspondence continuing with Godoy. As always, Gaspar argued his position clearly and calmly. Suddenly, in mid-November, another royal missive arrived announcing Gaspar's appointment as Minister of Justice in Madrid. Knowing that an old friend, released from prison, had interceded with Godoy for his reinstatement at the Court, he mused over the letter, wondering, *Do I see the hand of Cabarrús in this change of assignment?*

"It seems that I am to return to Madrid at last," he told Francisco quietly.

The day of his return to the capital, standing before the entrance to the Jovellanos home, Gaspar looked into his brother's concerned eyes and saw the deep flush of emotion in his handsome face.

"Do not worry, Francisco, I will be all right. It is my hope to be able to do some good for our countrymen and to be worthy of their affection and approbation."

Francisco de Paula breathed deeply and exhaled slowly. He looked intently at his brother. "Gaspar, you are going to give the tree a big shake, and many of the apples are going to be very angry. Be careful, *mi hermano*. Remember the vipers of which Saavedra warned you long ago."

Gaspar felt his chest swell with emotion. "I will take care, Francisco," he assured his brother and added, "I know you will look after the school and Robles in my absence. I do not know how long my tenure will be, and I am sure Robles will be happier here than cramped in a city stable."

Francisco nodded and followed Gaspar toward the waiting coach that would take him from the pleasant life he had enjoyed in Gijón. They shook hands, and Francisco wrapped his arms around his brother and held him tightly. "Courage!" he whispered, and Gaspar returned the hug. Then, he was off in a clatter of hooves.

At the rise of a hill near a large oak tree, the coach slowed. Gaspar looked back at his home and his beloved brother standing before it. He waved, and Francisco de Paula lifted a hand in answer.

CHAPTER TWENTY
The Unhappy Apples

aspar returned to his Madrid residence on a quiet, November afternoon. When no servant greeted him, he admitted himself to the dwelling and listened to the echo of his footsteps along the hallway to the drawing room.

The house seemed tended and in good order, and he was about to climb to the second floor, when he heard the front door swing open and the rapid patter of approaching footsteps.

A short, chubby, dark-haired man appeared in the doorway, both arms encumbered with grocery sacks.

"A thousand pardons, _señor_ Jovellanos," he gasped, out of breath from his hurried entrance. "I expected you this evening. I am so sorry that I was not here to greet you."

"_Está bien_," Gaspar said kindly. "May I assist you with your burden?"

"Oh, no, no, _señor_, _gracias_," he paused, collecting himself. "I am Diego. I am a _Madrileño_."

"_Mucho gusto, Diego_. I am pleased to meet you," Gaspar smiled, grateful once more to Saavedra for providing an assistant for him.

The man turned toward the kitchen and stopped. "Señor, there is a correspondence for you on the desk. It arrived this morning."

Gaspar sat at his old desk and smiled, recognizing the
handwriting on the letter. Francisco de Goya welcomed
him back to Madrid and looked forward to greeting him in
his studio at his earliest convenience.

"I look forward to that, too," Gaspar said aloud. The
responsibilities of his new position, however, would prevent a reunion with his friend for several weeks.

The following day, Gaspar accompanied Cabarrús to
a reception hosted by King Carlos IV and Queen Maria
Luisa at the Escorial, a palace near Madrid, and spent the
ensuing weeks in his new office submerged under paper-
work. He was aware that in working for reforms, he was
giving the tree a big shake, and as his brother had foretold,
many opposed and resented him. A visit to Goya provided
the only relief from his daunting workload.

*   *   *

One sunlit afternoon, leaving his work behind him,
Gaspar climbed the stairs to the artist's studio.
Francisco, thrilled to see his old friend, urged him
inside. They sat at the little table in the studio to drink coffee and talk.

"How happy I am to see you, Gaspar!" the artist
smiled.

"It has been a while, *mi amigo*," Gaspar said slowly,
aware that Francisco watched his lips. As they continued
to chat, he faced him and endeavored to speak naturally,
while carefully articulating each syllable. At one point,
noticing his friend's confusion, he used the hand alphabet
to complement his comments.

Francisco threw back his head and laughed heartily, delighted at Gaspar's signing and thrilled that his friend had taken time to learn the language of the deaf.

When Gaspar rested his head on a hand, Goya observed, "You seem tired, my friend. Are you working too hard?"

Gaspar smiled and straightened. "There is much to do and considerable resistance to my efforts." He glanced about the studio. "I see you have been busy as well.

"I have had many portrait commisions, and I thank you, Gaspar, for the recommendations you have sent to me." The artist stared at his weary friend a moment before standing and leafing through a pile of sketches. Selecting one, he returned to the table and passed it to Gaspar.

"Does this remind you of anyone?" he asked with a smile.

Gaspar gazed at the sketch and grinned. "You drew this a long time ago, Francisco. I was off to Salamanca, and you were finishing paintings for Godoy." He smiled at the accuracy of the artist's sketch of him. "I would like to commission a portrait, but, of course, you are very busy."

"I would find time to paint your portrait, Gaspar," Goya said without hesitation. "You could come here whenever you were free. I would put my other work aside to ac-comodate your schedule, and we would have time to talk while I worked."

*   *   *

A few days later, Gaspar arrived in mid-afternoon for his first portrait sitting with Francisco.

"*Excelente*," the artist approved, noticing his elegant gray jacket, black pants, white shirt, vest, and stockings. "Would you prefer to wear a formal wig?"

"Absolutely not," Gaspar answered a bit abruptly, and Goya raised his eyebrows. "Forgive me, Francisco, I have had a strange day." He passed a hand over his forehead.

"Are you well, Gaspar?" his concerned friend asked.

"Yes, yes, it is nothing...an ailment of the stomach that has bothered me since I dined at the Escorial."

Goya raised his eyebrows again. "What did you eat?"

"I can't remember, Francisco. It was weeks ago. Shall we begin?" Gaspar asked, endeavoring to change the subject.

"*Sí, por cierto.* I would like you to sit here, if you please, and we've definitely decided against a wig?" the artist confirmed.

"Yes, I'll just brush my hair," Gaspar grinned, "I don't want to look like a wild man from Asturias in your painting."

He settled into the chair, and Goya, standing before a large canvas, began to sketch. Gaspar remained silent several minutes, his dark eyes brooding and faraway. Francisco peered at him, concerned over the change in his usually relaxed and affable friend.

Catching Goya's eye, Gaspar spoke to him. "I accompanied Cabarrús to lunch at the home of Godoy earlier today," he began.

Goya stared at him. "Did you eat anything there?" he asked.

Gaspar sighed. "I was too oppressed in spirit to eat, drink, or say anything."

Goya watched his friend's face, waiting for him to continue.

"I was surprised at the guest list," Gaspar explained. Standing, he began to pace the room. Goya held his pencil suspended over the sketch, bewildered, until his friend paused before him.

"Godoy's wife was present, the Countess of Chinchón, lovely, beautiful, seated at the table beside him," Gaspar continued, "and on his other side was his friend, the woman we first saw years ago at the Royal Reception, Pepita Tudó." Gaspar drew breath and exhaled slowly. "There are few times when I have been at a loss for words, Francisco, but unable to speak, eat, or drink, I left Godoy's house, no doubt insulting our esteemed prime minister." Noticing his friend's suspended pencil, Gaspar sat down. "I'm sorry, Francisco. Please continue."

Gaspar fell silent and the artist's work at last progressed.

"I am not one of the Queen's favorites, Francisco," Gaspar commented, standing at the end of his first portrait sitting. "I am incapable of adulation. I cannot flatter anyone, nor fawn on those in authority. I do not tell the Queen of vacancies in the ministry, because I have no desire to consider her recommendations, and she resents me for it." He turned back at the door. "Francisco, I need reformers to work with me, not flatterers who think of their own positions and welfare, rather than the good of our people." He paused, his face serious. "I have many enemies, who resent me intensely."

Goya looked thoughtfully at his friend. "Gaspar, be careful where and what you eat and drink. We live in dangerous, turbulent times."

Gaspar met Goya's concerned gaze and grinned. "Did we have a good first sitting?" he asked. "Did you accomplish much?"

Goya laughed. "Next time I will secure you to the chair!"

*   *   *

Gaspar sat in the darkened drawing room contemplating his friend's warning.

Should I be concerned for my life? he wondered. *Have my attempts at reforms so upset my enemies that they are desperate to be rid of me?*

Gaspar knew that the publication by the prestigious Economic Society of his *Report on Agrarian Law*, which favored changes in land usage to increase productivity and improve the standard of living of Spain's poor, had rankled landowners. Likewise, his attempts at ending the practice of *mortmain*, the bequeathal to the Church of land that could be neither sold nor relinquished and usually lay uncultivated, had aggravated ecclesiastics, while his reforms of University studies, in which he urged instruction in Spanish rather than Latin, had angered scholastics. *My enemies are numerous and diverse*, he reflected.

He knew, also, that his attempts to abolish the Office of the Inquisition, arguing particularly against its ban on foreign books and ideas, had placed him in opposition to individuals of enormous power.

And in addition to all that, Gaspar smiled wryly, *the Queen can't stand me, and Godoy resents me and the loss of power my return has caused him.*

*   *   *

Gaspar continued to sit for his portrait, managing to stay seated, even as he discussed the intrigues and conspiracy he felt building around him at the Court.

"Are you feeling better?" Goya asked.

"Yes, my doctor prescribed a daily drink of olive oil, and over time it has provided some relief."

When Gaspar fell silent, Goya let his skillful brush move rapidly over the canvas, his oils adding color and vibrancy to his composition.

"How do you get on with the King and Queen?" Gaspar asked Francisco during a pause in the sitting.

The artist hesitated and smiled sheepishly. "They're crazy about me," he said quietly, and Gaspar laughed. "I paint their portraits, and they love sitting for me. I paint them honestly as I see and understand them, and they either don't notice or don't seem to care."

*   *   *

One afternoon, nine months after his return to Madrid, Gaspar climbed the stairs to his friend's studio. "I'm dismissed," he said simply. "I am returning to Gijón. My enemies have pressured the King, and I am dismissed."

Goya stared incredulously at his friend, and Gaspar forced a weary smile. "I have been replaced by a man completely opposed to reforms."

"You are leaving me amid the turmoil," Goya said quietly, struggling to conceal the distress his friend's announcement had caused him.

"Francisco," Gaspar said kindly, "you can get past any obstacle. I have always believed that." He turned to leave and looked back at the artist, "*Adiós, mi amigo.* May God allow us to meet again one day soon."

As the coach made its way through Asturias and Gaspar saw again the beloved green of his homeland, the elms, chestnuts, poplars, ashes, and oaks, his joy was tempered, his heart saddened. In the days before his departure, he

had learned of his brother's passing. Gaspar was returning
home, but too late; Francisco de Paula was gone.

CHAPTER TWENTY-ONE
The Countess of Peñalva

L
onely, missing his brother deeply, Gaspar busied himself with his school and filled his hours with work. On a mission to survey land cultivation, irrigation techniques, and mining operations in the region, he rode Robles southward from Gijón through the Asturian countryside to Leon and Oviedo. He looked forward especially to a visit in Oviedo at the home of the Countess of Peñalva, who was his sister, Benita.

The weather sunny, the air crisp, his sojourn through the countryside proceeded pleasantly. Along the way, he noted the natural beauty of the landscape, the architecture of churches and municipal structures, and the conditions of the inns, each night adding his day's observations to his *Diario*.

The final stop on Gaspar's itinerary was the elegant country home of his sister and her family. Benita, eleven years his senior, threw her arms around her brother, who, overjoyed to see her, hugged her tightly.

Arm in arm, they toured her gardens, lush with flowers and fruit trees and her stable. Benita always admired horses, and Gaspar complimented her on the quality of her animals.

"The Count will join us for dinner this evening," she explained, her lovely, radiant face framed with amber curls, here and there touched with gray. "I have asked our cook to prepare a feast for you, my darling brother." She beamed at him. "We will have some neighbors in afterwards, if all right with you. They are anxious to make your acquaintance." Gaspar smiled his approval.

Together, they sat, brother and sister, taking lunch and talked all afternoon in the cool shade of a garden tree, sharing childhood memories and stories. Late in the day, the Count returned to welcome Gaspar to his home while neighbors arrived for conversation and the evening meal. Benita's cook prepared trout, stewed vegetables, and sweet cakes for the dinner party, and the lively evening passed pleasantly for Gaspar.

Later, retiring to his room, he picked up a book but unable to concentrate, strolled out to the garden aglow with moonlight. The great house hushed, he sat on a wooden bench staring at the stars.

A glimmer of candlelight at the kitchen door drew his attention. "Gaspar, are you all right?" his sister whispered.

Gaspar smiled. How often in his childhood had his older sister checked on her little brother. "Benita," he said softly, "I am fine."

"Gaspar, I am sorry. I did not wish to disturb you. I wanted only to be sure that..."

"...I am all right," he finished her sentence, still smiling. "Come over and sit for a while."

Benita brought her candle and sat beside him on the bench.

"Can you not sleep?" she asked.

"Too many thoughts," he answered.

Benita placed the candle on the bench and folded her hands in her lap. "Tell me," she said quietly.

Silent a moment, Gasper gathered his thoughts. "Benita," he began, "I have failed in much of what I have tried to do and have made enemies. Twice, I have lost my position in Madrid and been sent, disgraced, into exile." He paused. "Your brother is back where he started and has little to show for his efforts."

When Gaspar fell silent, Benita breathed deeply, exhaling slowly. In the soft glow of candlelight, she began to speak quietly, a gentle firmness in her voice.

"Gaspar, you are and have always been my hero. Every gift that God has given to you, you use to the fullest. You work unselfishly for the good of your people and your country. You feel, for whatever reasons, that you have failed in your efforts, but, Gaspar, when we go forth in life, we never know how many lives we will touch, nor how we may influence or change them." She paused to breathe. "When something happens to you, when your dreams, and hopes, and efforts are in flames, you keep going, and, Gaspar, when you remain standing amid the ashes of defeat, you bring honor to all of us."

Listening to his sister, his heart swelled, and Gaspar blessed her silently.

"Good Night," Benita said gently, and taking her light, returned to the house.

*   *   *

The morning of his departure from Oviedo, he found his sister in the drive, her small, fine hands stroking and caressing Robles's head.

"When you find another like this one, Gaspar, please send him to me." She stepped forward to embrace her brother, who wrapped her in his arms and kissed her curly head.

"Take care, my darling sister," he whispered.

"*Tú, también*," she replied, her voice strong with emotion.

Gaspar and Robles traveled home to Gijón along winding roads, through hills and vales green with oaks and elms and orchards of fruit trees. Riding along, listening to the saddle creak, the thud, clop of horse hooves, and the wind in the treetops, Gaspar's thoughts turned to Goya.

When will I see my friend again? he wondered.

CHAPTER TWENTY-TWO
In the Dark

Striding toward the Institute, Gaspar saw late after-noon clouds gathering overhead. *A storm from the northwest*, he mused. The wind was increasing.

The librarian, hearing his approach, looked up nervously.

"Good Afternoon, Juan," Gaspar said, smiling. "I am returning the book I borrowed."

The man fumbled some papers, knocked a pen from its inkwell, and looked at Gaspar with troubled eyes.

Gaspar, perplexed at the odd behavior, asked, "What is it, Juan?" He followed the direction of the man's nervous gaze.

From behind a shelf, a tall figure, volume in hand, approached the librarian's desk. Dark hair and beard streaked with gray, he stared at Gaspar, and an icy voice inquired, "Under whose authority did this book become part of the library?"

Gaspar's recognized the book, an imported collection of scientific theories, and felt his face go warm. He met the man's eyes evenly and replied calmly, "I am Gaspar Melchor de Jovellanos. The Institute is my school. Any book found in this library is here with my approval."

"This is a foreign book. It is inappropriate and must be removed at once." Despite his efforts to remain calm, Gaspar's face and neck went red. His gaze not budging from the cold, hard face before him, his voice was quiet but firm, "The book remains in this library. Would you be so kind as to give it to the librarian."

Fingering the book, the man eyed Gaspar a long moment before dropping it with a thud on the librarian's desk.

"The Office of the Inquisition will be displeased, *señor* Jovellanos," the cold voice replied, and without further word the man walked from the room.

Gaspar could hear the dull thump of blood in his ears but turning to the librarian, whose face had gone very pale, managed with effort to speak in his usual calm tone.

"Here is the book I am returning, Juan. Thank you for finding it for me." He turned to leave.

"*Perdón, Gaspar,*" the man's agitated voice stopped him. "He seems dangerous. Will he cause trouble for the Institute?"

Gaspar smiled grimly. "He will not interfere with this school," he said firmly.

Gaspar sat at the dinner table unaware of his meal's content or taste, while the librarian's words echoed in his thoughts. *Will he cause trouble for the Institute?* He had worked hard to bring diversity to the Institute's library, importing many books for its collection, but he knew that even as his students demonstrated excellent progress, some in Madrid were highly critical of the educational theories and practices employed at the school and of his opposition to book censorship.

Watching him eat and fearing for his digestion, Clothilde brought him lemon water. Thanking her, Gaspar sipped it by the fireplace in his room. He was aware, deep within, of a growing unease.

*　　*　　*

The days in Gijón gliding by quietly, the incident in the library faded from Gaspar's memory, and he continued to enjoy his daily routine. The Institute was his particular pleasure, and he continued to teach classes at the school.

He looked forward, as always, to the mail delivery and was at his usual place before the fire one afternoon when Clothilde brought it to him. In the distance, he heard the low rumble of an approaching storm. Sorting through the correspondence, he selected a letter from Saavedra. Gaspar missed his friend and benefactor and longed to speak with him.

His eyes worked their way eagerly through the fine handwriting. Juan Arias was well, missed him, wished he were in Madrid, where he felt he was needed. The city was in a state of confusion, the mood of the Spanish Court affected by the Reign of Terror in France where the guillotine was very busy.

Gaspar frowned. *Madness and violence*, he thought, *What good can come of it?* He continued reading. A young general, successful in battle, had come to Paris and in the chaos seized power. His name, Napoleon Bonaparte.

Saavedra's letter concluded with a warning to his friend. He wrote of anonymous letters circulating through Spain, accusing Gaspar of disloyalty and portraying him as an enemy of the Throne and the Church. Fear, easily aroused and contagious, especially in times of turmoil and tumult, was rampant in Europe, and the powerful felt threatened. Saavedra advised Gaspar to be careful.

Watching the embers fade in the fireplace, he mulled over Saavedra's ominous words and closing his eyes, thought of his brother. "Francisco, the apples are still unhappy," he whispered.

*   *   *

The Asturian night was starless. Thick clouds covered Gijón, and in the distance thunder rumbled. Gaspar, asleep in his darkened room, heard the storm in his dreams. Stirring, he breathed deeply and rolled over, pulling his blankets about him.

A clatter of hoof beats roused him, and he was on his feet, when the soldiers entered his room. Shocked by their boldness, he struggled to control his anger and to think clearly.

"What is it? By what authority do you enter this house?"

"By orders from Madrid." The voice was harsh. "You are to come with us at once. Get dressed."

Gaspar, standing motionless, realized the futility of resistance. His enemies had done their work. He dressed, put a few items of clothing in a satchel, and left the house, while two of the soldiers remained to ransack his room and collect his writing and papers. A coach waited in the drive.

He stood calmly, surrounded by soldiers, before his house "Where am I going?" he inquired of the rough voice. "What is my destination?"

"You will know when you get there."

Gaspar turned and saw Felipe rush from the house, dazed from sleep.

"*Señor* Jovellanos, what is it?" he asked, bewildered and trembling. "What is the trouble? Where are they taking you?"

"Do not worry, Felipe. I will be all right. I am in exile now. I am only going a little farther away."

Rough hands pushed Gaspar toward the coach. One step up, he turned to smile at the trembling boy. Felipe raised a hand, and Gaspar waved back.

The coach was off in a rattle of gravel and hoofbeats, and Gaspar watched Felipe and the gentle life he had lived in Gijón fade away in the distance.

CHAPTER TWENTY-THREE
Exiled

The port of Barcelona was clogged with vessels, military and commercial, including a brig which would carry Gaspar Melchor de Jovellanos to exile on the Island of Majorca in the deep blue Meditteranean Sea.

He stood on deck for a long time, watching the coast-line of his beloved country drift away from him. A small bag of clothing his only possession, he was forbidden to carry books, paper, or writing materials.

On the trip from Gijón eastward to Barcelona, no visitors had been permitted to see him, nor news of the outside world given to him. Only by eavesdropping on his captors had he learned that Saavedra had been sent to his home in Jadraque and that Ceán Bermúdez remained in Seville.

When will I see my home and my friends again? he wondered, before pushing the thoughts from his mind. *Courage!* his brother had said, and that was what he needed now. He was determined to face this new challenge and somehow to prevail over it. A mild breeze from the water caressed his face while sea birds cried overhead.

I am a danger to my country, he mused, gazing back over the blue toward Spain. *I am a danger only to the self-absorbed fools that surround the king.* He pressed his lips together, disgusted. *My ideas threaten them. They are afraid to lose their comfortable, profitable niches. They are worthless...*

His agitation increasing, he paced near the railing while a guard eyed him warily.

They need not fear me. The threat will come from France, and the king and queen and Godoy and all of the court flatterers will be helpless against it.

He raised his face to the Mediterranean sun, hoping its warmth would calm his thoughts and soothe a troubled soul.

✳   ✳   ✳

Arriving in Majorca in the evening, Gaspar was transported to the island's Carthusian monastery, his prison in exile. He stood in a second-floor doorway, surveying his whitewashed, stuccoed cell, its narrow bed, wooden chair, and desk. A single window, open and unscreened, overlooked a garden and small orchard.

Fatigued from travel, he walked directly to the bed, tossed his jacket over the chair and removing his boots, collapsed on the mattress, which was straw-stuffed and, to his considerable relief, clean and *chinche* free.

Closing his eyes, his weary body, accustomed to the motion of the sea, felt the bed rocking beneath him. Exhausted, he fell into a deep sleep.

Hours later, he lay listening to the silence of the monastery. The bed no longer rocking, he opened his eyes slowly to light streaming through the window. *It must be midmorning*, he thought. Seeing something on the desk, he raised himself and walking to the window, found slices of bread, a small dish of honey, and a teapot, lukewarm from waiting for him.

Gaspar poured a cup and drank the tepid liquid thirstily. Brewed from herbs, it tasted pleasantly of citrus. From the open window, he saw monks in long robes and wide-brimmed, straw hats hoeing furrows of sprouting vegetables under a bright sun.

Hungry, he turned to the bread and honey and as he ate, looked about his sparsely furnished room. *It would seem that I have returned to the religious life*, he mused. Glancing at the wooden door, he reached a hand to the knob. *Locked, I suppose.* To his surprise, it turned.

Quickly finding his boots, Gaspar stepped quietly into the deserted hall. Walking slowly, his footsteps amplified by the stillness, he peered through an open doorway. Candles flickered near a gilded box on an altar. Nodding, he moved past the chapel and continued cautiously down the hall. His hand on a rough wooden balustrade, he descended a narrow stairway to ground level, where a large arched portal opened to the sun-splashed garden.

Stepping into the brilliance, Gaspar expected to be detained and returned upstairs. His arrival seemed unnoticed, however, and he strolled nonchalantly a few steps along the outer stuccoed wall of the monastery until he reached a small wooden bench. Squinting in the sun, he sat watching the monks at their labors.

If there is a rule of silence, he thought, *I may not hear a human voice for a very long time.* Contemplating this possibility, a familiar face returned to him. *How is Goya?* he wondered. His emotions stirring, Gaspar realized that thoughts of home and of his former life unsettled him. *If I am to survive in exile*, he reasoned, *I will have to put memories aside and deal with my present life, day by day.*

A hoe leaning against the garden wall caught his eye. He took it, walked to the nearest furrow of seedlings, and began to cultivate the dark, rich earth around them. Within minutes, he was aware of the sun on his back. His loosely-fitted, white shirt clung damply to him, and beads of perspiration trickled down his face. *A hat would help*, Gaspar thought. Nevertheless, he toiled on, aware that physical exertion eased his troubled thoughts.

He finished several furrows, before replacing the rake against the wall. Passing an arm across his forehead, he noticed a small stone well in the center of the garden. He lifted a bucket of cool water, took a long drink, and poured the remainder of the liquid over his head and down his back.

Dripping, refreshed, he surveyed the orchard saplings. *Lemon trees*, he thought and drawing another bucket, began to water them. The young plants drank thirstily, and Gaspar returned again and again to the well.

I shall have to think of a more efficient irrigation system, he mused, smiling at his primitive efforts. In his isolation, he was gratefully aware of sounds, birds in the orchard, water spilling from the bucket, his own breathing.

Well past noon, he looked up at last from his work to find the monks had vanished from the garden. Replacing the bucket at the well, he stopped to review his day's efforts, before returning to the monastery. Exhausted, his stomach rumbling, he climbed the stairs to his room, uncertain what to do next.

Perhaps I should look for the kitchen, he mused as he pushed open the door to his cell. "Ah!" he cried, surprised and delighted by the steaming dish of beans, two small fried fish, and a large chunk of crusty bread awaiting him on his desk.

Sitting at the desk, Gaspar bowed his head in gratitude. The fish were salty and crisp. Submerging a piece of bread in the bean broth, he waited for it to form a soft, spongy lump before plopping it into his mouth. He ate with gusto and when he had finished, leaned back contentedly in the chair.

A meal fit for royalty, he thought. *Simple food, like gold, better than gold after a day's work.* He lay on his bed watching twilight darken into night.

CHAPTER TWENTY-FOUR
The Snakes Bite

In the morning, Gaspar opened his eyes to find another breakfast of bread and tea on his desk. There was something else. He squinted at it from his bed before his curiosity drew him to the window.

A small pile of paper, a pen, and an inkwell. A smile crept across his face. "My work did not go unnoticed," he said quietly.

Something else. Writing on one of the sheets. He picked it up and read:

Señor Jovellanos,

Our library is located on the ground floor of the monastery. It is a small collection, but you are welcome to use it whenever you wish

He closed his eyes, breathed deeply, and whispered a prayer of thanks. Books, paper, ink. Treasures, truly treasures.

*　　*　　*

Sunlight streaming from a high window cast a golden glow over dust-covered books. *Clothilde should be here whisking everything clean*, Gaspar thought, before quickly returning his thoughts to the present.

121

Walking slowly along the shelves, he made mental notes of volumes to add to and enhance the library's collection. He was grateful for the sunlight. It helped his vision, which he realized was growing weaker.

A small cough startled him, and he glanced toward a corner in the room, where a monk, gaunt, gray, and bespectacled, sat poring over a book in his lap. Sensing Gaspar's gaze, he looked up, his bright, gray eyes peering inquisitively over the gold rims of his lenses.

Gaspar hesitated, not wishing to disturb him nor to intrude on his silence. The monk, however, solved his dilemma.

"May I help you, *señor?*" he asked, his voice surprisingly soft and mellow from such a bony man.

Gaspar relaxed. "*Perdoneme, por favor*, Father. I was just looking through your collection. I truly did not wish to disturb you."

The monk made a small waving gesture with a thin, wrinkled hand and slowly rising to his feet, tenderly placed the book on a shelf.

"No, no. No trouble at all. My name is Andrés, and if I am not mistaken, you are our guest, Gaspar Jovellanos."

Gaspar bowed, smiling to himself at his status as guest. "I thought, perhaps, there was a rule of silence."

"Yes, but I am free to speak when necessary and when I hike into the hills."

"Are you the librarian, Father Andrés?" Gaspar inquired.

"Yes, I suppose one could say that. I do try to look after the library, but I am primarily an apothecary. As you can surmise from the condition of this library, herbs and healing potions consume most of my time." He grinned a small crooked smile that revealed a gap between his front teeth.

Gaspar was intrigued. "Healing potions?" he repeated. "How do you prepare them, Father?"

A satisfied smile illumined the monk's face, as he realized at once that here was what he always enjoyed most, an inquisitive mind, and with it, a ready audience for his information.

"From herbs and plants that I find in the countryside here on Majorca," his voice continued warm and friendly, his eyes glittering happily. "I go into the hills once a week in search of them. Perhaps, you would like to accompany me, *señor* Jovellanos?"

"It would be my considerable pleasure, Father," Gaspar replied, "but I am not sure of my limits as a...a guest in the monastery."

The monk's smile widened. "I will see to it," he said simply. "If you wish to join me, I leave from the garden tomorrow after breakfast."

*   *   *

Gaspar climbed the hillside behind the monastery, taking notes as Father Andrés named plants and explained their medicinal uses. He was able to write with ease, his vision improving in the bright sunlight.

Walking and chatting with the elderly monk, Gaspar grew convinced that the man's wealth of botanical knowledge should be recorded and saved in a reference book.

"I am not much of a writer," the monk protested.

"We can perhaps collaborate, Father," Gaspar continued, his voice gently persuasive. "Together we could write a guidebook of medicinal plants and herbs, which would be a practical and valuable addition to the library." He grinned, as the old man, eyes glittering, smiled and nodded his agreement.

The two continued their pleasant meander in search of herbs among the vegetation of Majorca. From the crest of a hill, Gaspar looked out over the tranquil aquamarine water below him and, farther out from the island, the deep inky blue of the Mediterranean. His shirt, opened at the throat, billowed in the gentle seabreeze that drifted up the hill, stirring the languid, leafy branches of nearby trees.

∗ ∗ ∗

The sun warm on his face and the air sweet from drying grass, he sat on the sloping hill, his arms crossed on his knees. For the first time in many long days, his inner anguish dissolved, and he felt suddenly free, alive, breathing again.

He was content with the tranquillity of his life far from the Spanish Court, its intrigues, and enemies. He had books, paper, and ink. *I can be happy here*, he thought, *writing, reading, and sharing in the simple life of the monastery, close to nature and working for my daily bread. I will put Madrid and my enemies behind me forever and be at peace.*

The elderly monk, seeing his companion lost in thought, and sensing the grief that exile must have caused this brilliant scholar and distinguished statesman, remained quiet, not wishing to disturb him.

The days on Majorca continued happily. Gaspar, adjusting readily to the rhythms of monastic life, attended services with the monks, worked in the garden and orchard with them, explored the hills and meadows with Father Andrés, and read and wrote by candlelight long into the night. Living and working in community with the monks, he quickly became a much liked and appreciated guest of the monastery.

He had put the past behind him. Unfortunately, there were those who could not forget him, nor leave him undisturbed. A letter from Saavedra addressed to the monastery's abbot and given to Father Andrés carried another warning for Gaspar.

A copy of a book, *The Social Contract*, by the Frenchman, Rousseau, containing handwritten remarks complimenting Gaspar Jovellanos had been placed directly into the king's hands. The favorable mention of his name in a book feared and despised by many as helping to cause the French Revolution, was unfortunate and perilous, and Gaspar realized that his enemies still worked against him.

Awakening one morning to a familiar clatter of hooves, he stood at the window looking at soldiers in the garden and thinking of his friend and benefactor.

"You were right, Juan Arias," he said softly, "The snakes are still biting."

The soldiers had come to transfer him from the monastery to Bellver Castle, a more secure location on the island for such a dangerous man and far less hospitable than the home he had enjoyed with the monks.

The Carthusians assembled to bid their friend farewell. Gaspar said his good-byes under the cold glare of the impatient Captain of the Guard.

Father Andrés, his thin face bathed in tears, could not speak less he lose his composure completely. Gaspar smiled at the old man and through the tears, the monk's kind, unblinking gray eyes fortified him.

"*Hasta la vista, mi amigo, y muchas gracias por todo,*" Gaspar whispered in his elegant Castellano, also guarding his composure. "Until we meet again, my friend, many thanks for everything."

"God protect you, Gaspar," Father Andrés whispered.

Gaspar grasped the wrinkled hand extended to him, his fingers closing around a small package the monk passed to him. He placed it quickly, unseen, into his jacket pocket. Then, he was off again in a clatter of hoof beats.

*   *   *

Bellver Castle, a large stone structure on a hill, over-looked the island's harbor. In the courtyard, the tall, muscular Captain of the Guard looked at his prisoner with cold eyes, his face twisted in a sneer.

Gaspar met the man's gaze evenly, recognizing in it the resentment and anger that the uneducated and poor too often felt toward those perceived as nobility. Although sickened by the captain's attitude, he betrayed no emotion. *Courage!* his brother's voice whispered to him.

I will face this challenge calmly, he told himself, *one day at a time, for however long it will last.*

His new chamber had a narrow bed against a wall and a small window, which afforded little light to the room. Alone in his cell, the distress of his latest move and the separation from his friends momentarily overwhelmed him, and he sank down on the hard bed.

Whenever something happens, you keep going, Benita's gentle words flickered through his thoughts.

Opening the satchel he had carried from the monastery, he removed paper, a pen, and ink. *I will begin a report on educational reform at once*, he decided, the captain's behavior having intensified his belief in the need for education for everyone.

In the dim room, his weakened eyes squinted at the paper. *Light. I will need more light. I cannot work without light. I will need many candles.*

His frustration rising in the dark, chilly cell, he pulled his jacket tightly about him. Something brushed against his hand, and reaching into his pocket, Gaspar removed the small package Father Andrés had given to him. Pushing aside the paper wrapping, he saw a pair of gold rimmed lenses.

He stared at the glasses a moment before carefully, with trembling hands, placing them over his eyes and fixing the gold wires behind his ears. He opened his notebook and glanced at his handwriting. Offering a silent prayer of gratitude for his friend, Gaspar smiled. In the dim light, he could read.

CHAPTER TWENTY-FIVE
In the Well

Gaspar lay shivering in the early morning air. Spring had come to Majorca, and although the May days were brilliant with sun and warmth, his cell in Bellver Castle remained chilly until the noon sun turned it into an inferno.

He had adjusted to the routine of the castle and spent the weeks and months endeavoring to keep his mind alert. He worked on his education report and wrote descriptions of the castle's architecture and history. A priest, visiting the castle each week, located relevant books for him on the island.

As time elapsed, the Captain of the Guard's hostile attitude remained unchanged. Gaspar accepted the man's tedious behavior, calmly enduring his ordeal, determined to survive all humiliation and mistreatment.

Restricted from leaving the castle, he missed his lifelong habit of daily walks and the fresh air and exercise they afforded him. Over time, he became aware of an ache in his right hand and arm, often in his leg, and had begun to use a walking stick for support, when ambling about the castle.

He was aware, too, that his clothing, old and faded, hung on his always slim, but now gaunt body. His throat had been sore for several days. He was troubled most, however, by a cough that plagued him day and night. He wondered if he would ever recover his lost health.

He swung his legs over the side of the bed and with considerable effort, sat up. Shivering badly, he pulled on his worn jacket.

Coughing again, he was attempting to stand, when the door of his cell flew open, banging loudly against the wall. The captain's sneering face appeared in the doorway.

"Get your things together immediately," he ordered, his rude voice cold with contempt, and added mockingly, "The gentleman is leaving."

*　　*　　*

Gaspar leaned on his walking stick at the vessel's railing, watching Majorca disappear in the haze. The small satchel at his feet held his papers, a few books, some threadbare clothing, and a pair of gold-rimmed reading glasses, everything he owned after seven years of exile.

It did not matter. Nothing mattered. He was free, released by royal decree. He was returning to the mainland.

He sat down on the deck, pressed his back against a wooden barrel, and felt the movement of the vessel, as the breeze sent it along at a brisk pace.

"*Señor*," the brig captain interrupted his thoughts, "would you care to go below to rest in your cabin?"

Gaspar thanked him, but preferred remaining in the open air. The thought of going below bothered his stomach. Shivering, he pulled his jacket about him and passed a hand over his forehead.

I feel so cold, he thought, *yet I am burning hot. I will try to sleep.*

The vessel rolling gently side to side, he closed his eyes. His head swam, his stomach turned, and the world spun around him. Opening his eyes in a vain attempt to regain his balance, and leaning forward from the barrel, he listed to the left. Coarse boards whacked his face, and he lay dazed on the deck.

"There is a strong wind...We will put in at Barcelona..." The words reached his ears from somewhere far above him. "The royal family has left Madrid...The French general is in charge..."

His mind reeling, he was sitting at the bottom of a deep, cold well. *What a strange nightmare...* he thought, *...I need to sleep...I'm dreaming...*

* * *

He did not know how long he had slept, when he felt strong hands lifting him. Stirring, he tried to open his eyes. Arms lifeless, he breathed in short gasps. Wrapped in blankets, someone carrying him, he struggled in vain to clear his head and open his eyes.

I'm powerless, being taken God only knows where. Is it night or day? He tried again with all of his strength to rise from the well. After much effort, he heard his voice, but only as a groan.

"Easy, *señor* Jovellanos. Easy." Something in the voice that answered from far away startled him. He had grown unaccustomed to kindness. Giving up his struggle in the well, he lost consciousness.

* * *

Gaspar stirred without opening his eyes. He was traveling, jostling, and rocking. He heard the thunder of hoofbeats. His thoughts swimming...a loud whinny carried on the breeze...a great, gray stallion...

windmills. Swirling, sinking, the well revolved around him. He struggled against the dark. Suddenly, everything was silent, cold, and still.

From somewhere very deep and dark, Gaspar saw a light glistening, shimmering far above him. He was rising slowly, and as he did, the light grew larger. He breathed rapidly, breaths exhaled forcefully, struggling to reach the light, to leave the cold and the darkness, to escape from the well.

Suddenly, he was out. He heard his own panting breath. His head rolled from side to side. He was no longer cold. His face and body clammy and wet, someone was rubbing him dry with towels. He stared at the light that had grown very large. It turned toward him. A head, a hairless head.

A weak smile crept across Gaspar's exhausted face. "Pedro...Pedro."

"Don Gaspar, *Gracias a Dios*, your fever has broken. Please stay calm," Pedro entreated, his gentle voice, a warm breeze after bitter cold. "Do not try to speak, don Gaspar. You have been very ill. You are safe now."

"Where am I, Pedro?" Gaspar asked weakly. The kindly, little man placed a fresh, dry blanket over him and a pillow beneath his head.

"You are in Jadraque, *señor*, northeast of Madrid, in the home of your friend, don Juan Arias de Saavedra."

Gaspar smiled again, his head sinking into the soft feathers. He sighed deeply.

"*Gracias, Pedro*."

"Try to sleep, don Gaspar."

*   *   *

You can get past any obstacle, Francisco. His friend's words flickered through Goya's thoughts. He was grateful for the encouraging words, yet missed Jovellanos and wished he could speak with him.

The entry of French soldiers into Spain and the suffering of his countrymen, which the artist had witnessed, disturbed him profoundly, and to cope with his anger and fear, he immersed himself in his work. At the same time, he walked a fine line, carefully balancing his sympathy for the courageous Spanish resistance and his association with others, who believed the French would bring needed reforms to Spain.

Francisco was aware that the esteem in which he was held, the favor he enjoyed as Spain's leading artist helped him to survive the turmoil around him. *What would you say, Gaspar,* he wondered, *if you knew all that has happened in Spain?*

CHAPTER TWENTY-SIX
A Bonaparte Rules Spain

L ight from the villa's patio spilled through the open door, and the fresh spring morning beckoned to Gaspar. Under Pedro's care, he had improved, regained weight, and to his great relief, the persistent, tormenting cough was gone. Although stronger, he had not yet been on his feet unassisted.

Enough of this bed, he decided and pushing back the covers, sat up. He paused a moment before swinging his legs over the side. Reaching for his walking stick, he slowly stood and pulling on his dressing gown, walked cautiously toward the dazzle of light beyond his doorway.

Gaspar stood in the portal, gazing at the patio before him and breathing the sweet spring air. Sunlight filtered through budded branches, birds flitted and twittered in the trees, and grapevines clung to an arbor over a small wooden table and chairs.

Limping onto the patio stones, the stick supporting his right leg, he moved slowly toward the garden and orchard, his spirits rising with every careful step. Reaching the garden wall, he turned at a sound behind him and grinning happily, moved forward to embrace his beloved friend and patron.

"You are on your feet at last," Juan Arias beamed. "Pedro has kept me informed of your progress."

At that moment the elderly servant appeared carrying a breakfast tray. He came rapidly forward, mindful of the tray, and started in surprise at the sight of Gaspar standing in the patio. Quickly recovering, he placed the tray on the table.

"*Buenos días*, don Gaspar," he said politely. "Will you be taking breakfast outdoors this morning?"

"*Sí, Pedro, gracias.*"

Gaspar and Juan Arias sat at the table, while the little man carefully placed Gaspar's breakfast before him and unfolded his *servilleta*. There were slices of bread, thickly cut, a small pot of crushed berries in honey, and a glass of what appeared to be very thick, creamy milk. Gaspar hesitated.

"What is it?" he inquired politely of Pedro.

"*Leche de burra*," the little man replied.

"*Leche de burra?*" Gaspar questioned, his eyes widening.

"The milk of the donkey is a very old medicinal remedy," Pedro explained patiently. "It is rich and will help to strengthen you."

Gaspar raised the glass and peered at the milk tentatively. He put it to his lips and, after a moment's hesitation, sipped the creamy beverage. Pressing his lips together in a forced smile, he placed the glass on the table.

A broad grin lighted the face of Juan Arias. "Have you had enough of bread, honey, and *leche de burra*, my friend?" he asked. "Are you perhaps ready for something more substantial?"

Gaspar glanced at his friend with relief and gratitude. He was quite hungry and had, indeed, had enough of the *leche*.

"Pedro," Juan Arias continued, "Perhaps our cook has prepared something that would be a bit more fortifying for don Gaspar?"

Hesitating, the little man ran a critical, dubious eye over his patient. Gaspar smiled. Pedro had cared for him well since his arrival in Jadraque. Deeply grateful, he knew that he owed his recovery to him.

"Do you think that I could tolerate something more?" Gaspar asked quietly, deferring to the man's judgment. "I really feel a bit hungry...if you think I am ready..."

Pedro, pressing his lips together, made a decision. Picking up the tray and the *leche*, with a slight hint of indignation, he turned on his heel and vanished into the house.

Juan Arias sat watching the man with a bemused smile.

"That was kind of you, Gaspar, to leave the decision to Pedro."

"I owe my recovery to him, Juan. He seems these past days to have rarely left my side. He pulled me from the well..." Gaspar's voice drifted off as dark memories flickered in his mind. He cast them aside, seeing Pedro return with a second tray. This time, a steaming plate of beans and sausages, bread, and a pot of coffee were set before him. Gaspar laughed heartily.

"May I offer some of this to you, Juan?" he asked, fork in hand.

"No, no, *gracias*. I will content myself with the coffee."

Sniffing the steamy aroma, Gaspar was suddenly famished, and digging in, ate silently for several moments. When the sausages, thick with garlic, were gone and most of the beans, he tore a crust of bread to mop up the sauce. Putting the juicy mass into his mouth and swallowing, he took a long drink of coffee, before leaning back contentedly in his chair.

Pedro, having lingered to watch him eat, continued to eye him guardedly. As the little man turned back toward the house, Gaspar called after him in his soft, elegant voice, "*Gracias*, my friend." Hearing him, the servant paused before vanishing through the doorway.

His appetite satisfied, Gaspar turned his attention to Saavedra.

"Juan Arias," he began, reflectively, somewhat uncertainly, "when I was ill, adrift in the well of my sickness, I had a strange dream, a nightmare."

Saavedra eyed him over his coffee cup.

"What kind of nightmare?"

Gaspar was silent, rolling back pages of memory.

"In this dream, I heard two sailors talking. Their words were very strange, troubling. I heard that the king and queen were gone from Madrid." His memory clearing, Gaspar's words tumbled forth. "The French had come to the capital. A general ruled the city." He looked up from his empty plate and stared at his friend. "It was a nightmare."

Juan Arias met his gaze. "It was not a dream, Gaspar," he said quietly. "Much has happened since you have been away." Saavedra looked toward where the sun was filtering through his orchard. "Napoleon has seized power in France, and Spain is a jewel that he wishes to add to his crown along with all of her American possessions and the wealth that they provide."

Gaspar listened intently and watched his friend's face as he spoke.

"He is a brilliant leader," Juan Arias continued, "both as general and as self-crowned emperor." He leaned back in his chair, a hint of disgust in his dark eyes. "See what the revolution, the violence, and chaos have brought not only to France, but to Europe as well. What has been gained by murdering the monarchs? Those who espoused the guillotine have themselves fallen under its blade, and France is led by this man who would be emperor of the world."

Gaspar, eager to hear every detail of news he had missed in exile, waited patiently for his friend to collect his thoughts and emotions.

"How did the royal family come to leave Spain?" he asked at length. "How did French soldiers gain access to our country?"

"They were invited in," Saavedra said, a wry smile on his face and anger edging his voice, "by our esteemed minister, Godoy, who in exchange for allowing the French passage through our land to attack Portugal, was to receive a share of the spoils of war. Napoleon quickly seized the opportunity to send a hundred thousand soldiers to Spain along with his brother-in-law, Marshal Joachim Murat, as military commander."

Gaspar exhaled slowly. "Our king and queen and Godoy," he mused, "I sensed that trouble awaited them."

Saavedra stood and paced before the table, walking off the nervous irritation the topic was causing him.

"Prince Ferdinand, with an eye on the throne for himself, worked with Napoleon to remove his parents from power. For a brief time, he reigned as Ferdinand VII during which period his one sensible act was to return you from exile." Juan Arias resumed his seat at the table.

"Napoleon invited Carlos IV, Maria Luisa, and Godoy, along with the new king, to Paris to discuss politics," he continued, a tinge of sarcasm in his voice. "As a reward for Ferdinand's traitorous behavior, he was forced to remain in France, along with his parents and Godoy, and in place of the king, Napoleon sent his elder brother to occupy our Spanish throne." Saavedra sighed deeply. "All hail, King Joseph I. A Bonaparte rules Spain." He lapsed into silence, his eyes glazed, staring at the garden.

Absorbing this new information, Gaspar sat silently.

"And the people, the *Madrileños*?" he asked, at length, "how have they accepted this?"

"Some are working for and with the French," Juan Arias answered. "Yes," he continued, seeing the surprise in Gaspar's eyes. "Some, also from among the *ilustrados*, the enlightened ones, believe that the French will bring innovative thinking to our country, and the changes and reforms for which they have worked and would welcome. They are called the '*afrancesados*.'"

He took a long drink of his coffee. "Others resent the presence of Napoleon's brother. They prefer to have their own king, even a wretched, incompetent king would be better for them than Napoleon's man. The French soldiers have behaved brutally since their arrival in Spain, and a resistance has sprung up among our people."

Deeply interested in his friend's discourse, Gaspar felt keenly the time he had been away from the heartbeat of his country. He nodded, encouraging Juan Arias to continue. Pedro, however, returned to the patio, carrying a bowl of fruit, which he placed before the men, and a letter on a small silver tray, which he set before Gaspar.

"This arrived for you in the mail, don Gaspar," he said, before quietly retreating to the house.

Gaspar tore open the missive and read it quickly. Frowning, he reread it slowly, before tossing it back onto the tray and looking at Saavedra.

"It is from Cabarrús. It seems that King Joseph I has offered me a ministry position in his government."

Juan Arias's brows arched over eyes that widened in surprise and interest.

"It is an acknowledgment of your abilities and talent, Gaspar. Adding you to his administration would surely be a plum for the new ruler. He knows the respect you have earned from your countrymen. Even the fear and resentment of your enemies is a recognition of your strength and influence. It would be to his great credit to call you '*afrancesado*.'"

Gaspar pushed back his chair and raising himself, took a few steps toward the garden. He turned back, leaning on his walking stick, to look at Saavedra.

"I am Asturian," he said quietly. "*Soy español.*"

Juan Arias eyed his friend closely. "And your friend, Cabarrús?"

"He apparently believes that Spain's future lies with Napoleon. His loyalty is with the French."

"He has been our good friend," Juan Arias replied.

"It is for this friend that I suffered exile and disgrace to my name and reputation. It would appear that our connection is at last over." Gaspar paused to collect himself. "I will send my regrets to Bonaparte. My health will serve as an excuse and allow me time to plan my future."

"You need time to recover your strength," Saavedra corrected him, "before you decide on any action. You are welcome to stay here, Gaspar, for as long as you wish."

CHAPTER TWENTY-SEVEN
Goya's Story

Gaspar walked in Saavedra's garden each morning, enjoying the pastel lights of dawn amid rows of fruit trees and flowers, some spreading across the ground, others clinging to arbors. A path along a crumbling rock wall afforded him views of fields stretching toward the horizon and, far beyond, to Madrid.

This morning, he was thinking about the Junta Central, the insurgent Spanish government, which he had decided to join in resistance to the rule of Joseph I until Spain could rid herself of French occupation. Lingering at the rock wall, he did not notice Pedro hurrying toward him along the garden path.

"*Perdón*, don Gaspar." Excited, he needed to catch his breath. "You have a visitor."

Gaspar looked at him questioningly.

"Francisco de Goya is here to see you." Pedro, having regained his composure, read the delight in Gaspar's eyes.

Francisco, standing alone in the patio, turned at the sight of Gaspar's shadow on the stone floor. The two friends gazed at each other a moment, smiling, before stepping forward to grasp hands and embrace.

An unkempt mass of curls still surrounded the artist's plump face, while his dark, penetrating eyes seemed to Gaspar even more intense and watchful. They sat across from each other at the patio table, Gaspar beaming at his old friend who grinned at him in return.

"I have missed you, *mi amigo*," Gaspar said articulating his words carefully as Francisco watched his lips.

"I cannot tell you how many times you have entered my thoughts, Gaspar. During all of the turmoil, how many times I wanted to talk with you. Much has changed in the years you have been away. How your presence was desired by your friends! How you were missed by those who love Spain!"

The two friends wandered through the garden, chatting, and Gaspar felt his spirits rise with every moment shared with his old friend. Later in the evening, they joined Saavedra for supper.

Pedro, to celebrate the painter's arrival and the happy reunion of the three men, prepared a small banquet, carefully arranging heaps of fried trout and pickled salmon, a ragout of fresh vegetables, and stewed pears and cheese on the candlelit dining table. Afterwards, the three men retired to the coolness of the drawing room to sip brandy. From the doorway, Gaspar spied a large easel with a drapery covered canvas.

Francisco has brought a painting to share with us, he mused happily and stood with Juan Arias before the easel, as Goya slowly removed the drape.

"Ah!" Juan Arias exclaimed.

Gaspar stared in silence, his eyes riveted to the canvas. From somewhere faraway he heard Saavedra's voice. "You have captured our elegant friend magnificently... his head resting on a hand...the kind, intelligent eyes...the minister in his office bearing the burden of the challenges before him...papers piled on an ornate desk..."

His gaze fixed on Gaspar's face, Goya was unaware of the comments.

"A statue of Minerva, the Roman goddess of wisdom and the arts and sciences, occupies the upper right section," Saavedra's appraisal continued, "and offers a hand to the minister, while the light of truth floods in from the left, illuminating him. A brilliant and fitting composition, Francisco."

Gazing at his image on the canvas, Gaspar's thoughts drifted away to a candlelit ballroom, long ago, to a swirl of color, and a hum of voices. He remembered a young man's face, remarkable for the intense, piercing eyes that looked deeply into his to see what lived on the inside.

At last, Gaspar's gaze moved from the painting and met the artist's eyes, which glittered, a bemused smile lighting them. Goya waited for his friend to speak. Overwhelmed by the portrait and by the artist's perception of his inner struggle, Gaspar said quietly, "I am glad that I brushed my hair," and grinned at his friend who threw back his head and laughed heartily.

"*Gracias*, Francisco," Gaspar added, as they moved toward the drawing room chairs.

"It was my pleasure, Gaspar. I completed the canvas after your departure. I have another sketch, a standing pose, which I did toward the end of our sessions. I will share it with you another time."

Through the large doors open to the evening air, they watched twilight descend on the patio. Pedro encouraged a small fire on the hearth, while Saavedra listened with amusement and interest, as Gaspar and Francisco talked of past times, of cabriolet rides, royal soirees, and paintings.

As the conversation turned to politics, the men grew serious. Francisco had much to tell his friends, but emotions blocked him, and words would not come easily. He decided to let his work speak for him. Retrieving the sketches he had brought with him and setting them before the interested eyes of Gaspar and Juan Arias, the artist found his voice.

"At first, some in Spain thought that the French presence in the country would be helpful, but the soldiers shocked us with their savagery," he began.

Gaspar, silent, his dark eyes serious and intense, focused on Francisco's sketches. They were drawings of unspeakable barbarity and cruelty inflicted on his countrymen and women.

When he had viewed all of them, he lifted his eyes and gazed out at the patio. He understood the change in the painter's eyes, the hint of pain, sorrow, even outrage that now tinged them. Francisco's artist eyes, which by nature looked so closely at details, had witnessed things no human being should have to see. Goya had seen the horrors of war.

The fire crackling on the hearth, Gaspar turned to meet his friend's haunting gaze. "What is it, Francisco?" he asked quietly, "What else did you see? What happened?"

Before Goya could answer, Pedro came to close the drawing room doors and to light candles against the gathering darkness.

"Will there be anything else, *señor* Saavedra?" he asked.

"*No, gracias, Pedro. Buenas Noches.*"

The little man withdrew from the room. The candles and the crackling fire cast a golden glow on the faces of the men, providing a tranquil setting for the turbulent tale to be told.

Goya began his story, "You know that Napoleon had placed his brother on the Spanish throne, exiling Francisco VII along with his parents and Godoy to France. An order came for the removal and exile, also, of the king's thirteen-year-old son, who had remained behind in the palace." Francisco paused to breathe, color creeping into his face, as memories flooded over him.

"On the second of May, I was walking near the Puerta del Sol. It was a calm day. The sun was bright. I saw French soldiers, with the boy in hand, leading him toward a carriage. He did not want to go and resisted, struggled against them. The crowd of *Madrileños* saw this, and without hesitation men and women surged forward to help him." Goya's excitement building, his voice grew louder.

"With sticks and rocks and bare hands, they fought the French soldiers. When it seemed that the people would be successful, Napoleon's Egyptian mercenaries, the Mamelukes, arrived on horseback to beat off and destroy the *Madrileños*.

"They fought hard, hand to hand, often unarmed against swords and scimitars. I saw one Mameluke pulled from his great white horse, his red pantalooned legs stretched across the animal's back, a Spaniard's dagger raised above his chest. All was confusion and dust. There must have been screams and cries, because I saw many mouths opened wide."

Francisco paused to run a hand over his forehead. Gaspar and Juan Arias waited in silence for him to continue.

"They fought on bravely, savagely, shocking the Mamelukes with their intensity, their defense of the *Infante*. He was, after all, the son of their king. In the end, he was taken away, leaving behind a square littered with the dead and injured."

Gaspar, shocked by his friend's story, leaned forward toward him. "What happened to the people?" he asked in a low voice.

"The French were infuriated by the uprising, and Murat ordered the arrest of all who had participated in it," Francisco paused to stare into the gloom beyond the patio doors.

"The next night, the third of May, was starless, the sky overcast. I was in my studio, thinking of lighting candles and trying to work. I was restless, agitated and told Josefa that I was going for a walk.

"That night, I walked the dark, deserted streets of Madrid and in my silent world felt a loneliness, a desperation I had never known. Somehow, I lost my direction and seemed to wander blindly.

"Then, I passed the Cathedral of San Fernando and knew that I was approaching the hill of Principe Pio. I was drawn toward a strange light ahead of me, strange because the glow came not from above, but from the ground."

Francisco paused, placing his head in both hands and closing his eyes. Juan Arias brought a glass of water from the dining table to him, and he drank gratefully. Gaspar's eyes had not left the artist's face.

"Something, I do not know what," he continued, "something inside made me press myself against the wall of a house and peer round it, unseen, at what was happening on Principe Pio.

"I saw the light that had led me there, a lantern, a large box lantern at the feet of a row of French soldiers...seven of them...perhaps more. They wore long, gray overcoats, with swords at their sides, and tall black hats. They were hunched forward, their faces hidden.

"They aimed their rifles ahead...ahead at the men of Madrid, those who had fought the previous day. They came one by one in a long, ragged line, some with hands over their faces. One by one the rifles shot forth fire. I could hear nothing, but somehow felt each rifle shock deep within my bones. One by one, the pride and honor of Spain fell to the ground, their blood soaking the good earth. A priest held his crucifix before each martyr who fell.

"My stomach ached as if I had been kicked hard, and my head swam. I wanted to run fast from that scene. I bit my lip to control myself. I pressed my face hard against the rock wall of the house and took a last look at the horror.

"Under the black sky, I saw a *Madrileño*, white shirt open, bare chest exposed, a man, only a man. The rifles aimed. He threw his hands and arms up and out...brave...defiant...

"I turned and ran stumbling, falling, choking for air. I did not know where I was or how far from the hill I had gone, when I stopped in the dark and silence. I stood and sobbed as I have never in my life.

"When my head cleared and I could breathe again, I went home and sat alone the rest of the night in my studio."

In the flickering candlelight, the three men sat unmoving, silent. Francisco had finished his story.

CHAPTER TWENTY-EIGHT
Vaya con Dios

T he two friends spent the days of the artist's visit chatting from morning till night. When it was time for Goya to return to his studio in Madrid, Gaspar joined Juan Arias in the front drive of the villa and helped load his bags onto the coach.

The painter shook hands with Juan Arias, embraced Gaspar and climbed quickly into the coach. Once seated inside, he looked out the small side window at his friends.

"Get well, Gaspar," he said. "One day, I will be looking for you again in Madrid, where you are needed."

Gaspar put his hands on the open window frame of the coach and looked directly into Francisco's face.

"*Vaya con Dios*, you old bullfighter," he grinned at his friend.

The coach was off in a lurch, and Goya's laughter echoed back to the two men standing in the drive.

* * *

T he summer days slipped by enjoyably for Gaspar. His strength increased even as he realized he would always need some support from the walking stick. His love for reading and writing remained unchanged. Inspired by Goya and encouraged by Saavedra, he tried painting landscapes on the walls of his bedroom in Jadraque, in one scene depicting Bellver Castle as he remembered it, in another a farm in Castile.

Gaspar appreciated the quiet rhythm of his days, but deep within, as his vigor returned, he felt a growing restlessness. He wanted to be of service to the Junta, the underground government formed in resistance to Napoleon Bonaparte and to his brother, Joseph I. He wanted to work for the welfare of his country and to be of use to her people.

One fine summer morning, therefore, another coach waited in front of Saavedra's villa. Pedro carefully packed Gaspar's belongings and after placing them in the coach, stood quietly beside Juan Arias in the driveway.

"I am forever in your debt, Pedro," Gaspar said, facing the little man. "I owe my life to you."

Pedro looked straight ahead, avoiding Gaspar's eyes. He nodded, "I wish you well, don Gaspar. It has been my pleasure to serve you." They clasped hands.

Gaspar turned to Saavedra. Emotions welled within him, and he was unable to speak. Juan Arias broke the silence.

"You are everything I would have wished in a son."

Gaspar, meeting the man's gaze, seemed to see his friend and patron's face for the first time, the lines of age, the gray hair, and yet, the ever intense and brilliant eyes.

"Every time I have needed help, you have come to my aid. You have been my second father, and your strength and wisdom have supported my life." He paused to collect himself. "I would like you to have Goya's portrait," Gaspar added quietly, "to remember me."

"I will treasure it and keep it in your room until you return to us," Juan Arias answered.

They embraced, and Gaspar was off in a clatter of horse hooves and coach wheels. He was leaving his friends, but he would carry Juan Arias and Pedro with him in his heart forever.

The coach carried Gaspar south to Seville, to the city he had left years ago. He planned to work as a delegate from Asturias to the Junta Central, developing a plan for public education and helping to write a constitution.

When French soldiers approached Seville, he and the delegates from other provinces moved to Cadiz, a port city on the Atlantic Ocean, where they continued to represent the Spanish government in exile until Joseph I and Napoleon's occupying army withdrew from their country.

Eager to be of service to his countrymen, Gaspar devoted all of his energy to the tasks before him, but as the weeks and months passed, he became aware of a deeper desire. He longed to be home, to return to Gijón. He needed to see Asturias again. His body had strengthened. He needed to restore his soul.

Completing his work and learning that the French had left Gijón, Gaspar boarded a brig in the harbor and as a brisk breeze filled the vessel's sails, he stood on deck, his cloak ruffling about him, and watched the port of Cádiz vanish on the horizon.

CHAPTER TWENTY-NINE
Amid the Ashes

G aspar walked from the wharf and stood in the plaza early on a warm August morning. After seven years of exile, he had returned home unannounced. He turned and walked across the silent square.

The church was empty, cool, and tranquil. Proceeding slowly down the main aisle, his eyes rested on the flickering candles, and he gazed again, as in his childhood, at the wooden images peering at him from niches in the walls.

He ran his hand along the low iron railing. Opening the gate and stepping through, he walked slowly to stand before the gilded box on the altar. Dropping to his knees, head bowed a moment, Gaspar slowly lay face down, stretching out his arms in the cool dust of the marble floor.

"*Gracias, gracias,*" he whispered, "thank you for bringing me home."

Outside again, he walked as quickly as his right leg would allow in the direction of the Jovellanos house. He paused in the doorway before stepping inside, the last surviving member of a family that had once filled the house with life and laughter. He leaned on his walking stick, listening to the silence.

Standing in the hall, he breathed the air of home, felt the house around him, the caress of things familiar. Moving slowly down the passage, he noticed the good order and cleanliness of the house, the high polish of dark wood floors and furniture.

From the dining room doorway, he saw his brother's chair at the table, and his heart tightened, beating faster. He turned quickly and walked down the hall to his bedroom.

Looking at the fireplace and the two chairs before it, the silence of the house pressed hard against him, and he could hear his heart beat in his ears. He turned back toward the front door and walked into the plaza.

The air warming, Gaspar felt the morning sun on his face and neck. He forced his thoughts away from the empty house and directed his steps across the square.

"Education, education," he repeated to himself, "it is the answer and hope for everyone."

He stopped abruptly, startled by the facade of his school. All of the windows were broken, and shattered glass littered the ground. At his touch, the unlocked door groaned open.

A stench assailed Gaspar, and with it a flash of memories of a faraway prison in Seville. In his absence, French soldiers, commandeering the Institute, had used it as a barracks. One broken bench remained of the school's furnishings, the rest, no doubt, used for firewood.

Gaspar walked dumbly, blindly toward the library and from the doorway, viewed the devastation of his treasure. The shelves were stripped bare.

His mouth dry and a dull ache in his heart, Gaspar stood in his ruined school, silent, alone, unable to think.

Here amid the ashes of his dreams, he could see only the arrogant sneer of the Captain of the Guard. He turned and limped back to his home.

Standing before the front door of the Jovellanos house, where once every fiber of his being had longed to be, he sighed deeply. For seven years, to keep from weakening, he had wrestled with his thoughts, struggled to stop them from drifting always here. He had endured and returned to loneliness and defeat.

"Home at last," he said quietly.

A snort startled him, a stamped foot roused him. He glanced toward the stable. A horse whinnied, and Gaspar's heart quickened at the sound.

He limped across the corral, a smile creeping across his face as he approached the stall.

"Robles," he whispered. "Robles, old boy."

The great, gray horse nickered, nodded its head, and restless, snorted again. Feeling Gaspar's hands on his face, he settled and placing his muzzle on his master's shoulder, nibbled his arm.

Gaspar, smiling with joy, ran his hand down the horse's neck and flank, delighted to find the animal sleek and well-groomed.

"Robles, my old friend, you seem to have aged more gracefully than I," Gaspar, grinning, spoke quietly to the animal. "The House of Jovellanos has cared well for you."

Robles, nickering softly, continued to nuzzle his arm.

"Do you remember our adventures, old boy?" Gaspar's words began to tumble forth. "We were chasing windmills. We were going to right wrongs and make the world a better place." The ache swelled suddenly in his chest, choking his voice. His fingers tightened in the long hair of the horse's mane, and he pressed his face against Robles's neck. Tears came, tears for Francisco de Paula, and Benita, tears for his school, for lonely, bitter days of exile, and for lost and broken dreams.

Unmoving, Robles supported his master until he finally straightened, breathing slowly to calm himself. A gentle voice flickered in Gaspar's memory, *You are my hero...In the ashes of your defeats, you remain standing...you bring honor to all of us...*

He ran his hand again slowly along the beautifully arched neck.

"You are right, Robles, this is no way for a Jovellanos to behave. I must remember always the spirits of my sister and my brother." He smiled. "Courage, always, courage."

He ran his hand up the horse's face and forehead. "We will begin again, my magnificent friend. We are not defeated. We will begin again."

The great horse relaxed, stamped, flicked its tail, and reached for some hay.

CHAPTER THIRTY
The Lives We Touch

Gaspar returned to the Institute later that morning to assess the building's damage and to plan repairs. He was mulling over the need for window replacements and new bookshelves in the library, when he realized he was no longer alone.

In the doorway, a young man, tall, slender, fair hair neatly brushed, watched him closely. He wore a loosely-fitted white cotton shirt, breeches, and boots.

Gaspar, leaning on his stick, surveyed the young gentleman, his relaxed stance and steady gaze faintly familiar to him. "*Buenos días*," he said cordially.

"*Buenos días, señor* Jovellanos," the young man replied, emotion filling his voice, "*Gracias a Dios*, you are here."

Amazed, Gaspar stared into the deep blue eyes.

"Felipe?"

"*Sí, señor*," the young man approached, extending his hand. "It is I."

They walked, chatting, to the front entrance and finding a shaded spot, sat together on a rock wall.

"I studied here until the French came," Felipe explained, his voice tinged with disgust.

"I am going to restore the school, Felipe. The windows and doors will be replaced, and I will send for new benches." Gaspar's voice was firm, his enthusiasm growing with every word. "I will locate my teachers and students. Hopefully, if all goes well, the Institute will reopen in the autumn."

Felipe beamed with pleasure at Gaspar's words.

"*Señor* Jovellanos," he said quietly, "when I was studying here, I learned to speak French and English. I would like to continue to learn." He hesitated. "One day, I would like, if it would be agreeable to you, to teach here."

Gaspar looked at the young man for a long moment.

"Felipe," he said at last, "when you are teaching, remember that education is for everyone, boys and girls, regardless of rank or wealth. An educated populace is the strength of a nation."

Felipe glowed with pleasure at the endorsement of his dreams and rose, as Gaspar, leaning on his walking stick, lifted himself to his feet.

"And Felipe," Gaspar continued, as they turned toward the square, "never be afraid to let your students use their minds. Thinking...reasoning is a God-given talent that some try to suffocate, but it is as natural and as necessary to a human being as breathing. With it we can seek the light of truth; without it we remain in the dark where monsters can be produced."

In the sunny plaza, walking home together, Gaspar saw people approaching, smiling, hands extended, heard his name cried aloud and enthusiastic greetings.

"*Señor* Jovellanos!"

"Welcome home!"

"Our hero has returned."

"The father of our country is here."

Astonished by the attention lavished on him, Gaspar was at once embarrassed and thrilled.

"Thank God, you are home, *señor* Jovellanos," a neighbor greeted him. "Asturias has been a lonesome place without you."

They followed him home, chattering happily. Gaspar thanked them, invited them to visit him often, hoped to be able to stay with them many days.

In the kitchen awaiting his return, Clothilde and her husband, Domingo, beamed with pleasure when he entered with their son.

"*Señor* Jovellanos, welcome home," Domingo said earnestly. He was short, well-muscled with touches of gray in his curly, brown hair.

"I have prepared your lunch, don Gaspar," Clothilde said gently. She placed a plate of fried fish and stewed vegetables before him as he sat at the table.

Gaspar grinned at the three standing, smiling before him.

"You have cared well for the estate in my absence and with my brother's passing," he paused, "and I am deeply grateful to you." Gaspar looked at Felipe. "And Robles has obviously been treated as royalty, and for that, also, I thank you."

They continued to beam at him.

"It is good to be home," he said, and his heart was in his words.

That night, Gaspar sat on the front porch of the Jovellanos home with Clothilde, Domingo, and Felipe, listening to bells chiming and watching bonfires burning all over Gijón in celebration of his return.

In the morning, taking his daily *paseo* once again along the shore, with a strong, salty seabreeze ruffling his shirt, he saw in the harbor vessels adorned with festive pennants in his honor.

Amazed and deeply moved by the devotion and emotion of his countrymen, he looked out at the sparkling blue sea. *When we go forth in life...we never know the lives we touch*, his sister's words whispered to him in the wind.

As the days glided by, Gaspar, with the help of his neighbors, made good progress in restoring the Institute. His spirits reviving in the sweet surroundings of home and happy to be once again deluged with work, he took time to transfer ownership of a house on the Jovellanos estate to Felipe's parents.

Gaspar had hoped to spend many days in Gijón, but his wishes were thwarted. In November, shortly after the reopening of the Institute, word reached the city that French troops, returning to Asturias, were headed toward Gijón.

Gaspar's neighbors, alarmed for his welfare, warned him of the reported military advance. He knew that his alliance with the Junta in opposition to French rule in Madrid, would force him to flee at once or risk arrest, imprisonment, perhaps further exile.

He would leave by boat, taking little more than a cloak to protect against sea breezes and storms. Domingo would see him safely to Galicia, before making his own way home by land.

Felipe accompanied them to the wharf. From the gang-plank of the brig, Gaspar turned to the young man.

"Look after Robles," he said and shook hands.

Felipe nodded. *"Vaya con Dios, señor Jovellanos,"* he said. He embraced his father and was standing on the windswept wharf, as the vessel took the two most important men in his life out to sea. He wondered if and when he would ever see them again.

CHAPTER THIRTY-ONE
Starlight

The voyage was rough. One day out of port, a stiff gale blew in from the northwest, tossing the brig on a choppy, tormented sea and chilling the men aboard with an icy spray.

During the night, the wind continued ferocious, claiming as a victim one of the brig's masts. Under an angry, overcast sky, the captain struggled valiantly to maintain control of the creaking, moaning vessel, as it pitched and rolled dangerously close to the rocky coastline.

Gaspar, wrapped in his cloak against the cold, sat braced at the vessel's side, his feet pressed against the brig's planking. Domingo was near, watching him, taking courage from his calm face.

Toward midnight, the captain lost his battle with wind and sea, and the brig, lurching suddenly with a grinding thud, wedged itself between two large rocks. Taking on water, the vessel's position unstable, all hands were ordered to abandon ship at once.

The best hope for all was to climb, without delay, onto the rocks. Domingo and Gaspar clambered over the side of the vessel onto a large rock, which they discovered, with relief, was part of a wall leading back to shore.

In the darkness, the brig's human cargo made its way slowly and carefully, sometimes upright, other times in a crablike crawl, over the precariously wet rocks. Reaching shore, they pressed themselves into a cavelike opening in the sea cliff to await the storm's end and morning light.

Gaspar, breathing a bit heavily from the tortuous scramble, wrapped his cloak about him and sat out of the wind near the cave entrance, his back pressed against a wall. He watched calmly as Domingo and a sailor searched for firewood. Soaked through with sea spray, he shivered and coughed in the cold.

Looking out over the storm-tossed sea, Gaspar watched the clouds move eastward before the wind. In their place, a dazzle of stars filled the ink blue sky. The wind continued, waves crashed against the shore, but Gaspar sat watching starlight spread across the turbulent scene, gradually illumining the dark. He smiled.

✳   ✳   ✳

The balcony doors of the artist's studio were opened to the cool Madrid night. A single candle glowed in the workroom. Francisco de Goya arranged his colors on his palette. He would work tonight.

In the candle glow, he surveyed some drawings he had completed, reflections of Spanish life and society, ideas he had discussed with Gaspar. His gaze drifted to his bullfight sketches. He was smiling, remembering his friend's critique of them, when a sudden breeze from the balcony ruffled his shirt and snuffed out the candle.

Startled, he stood in the silent darkness. He walked to the balcony and lifted his head to the breeze that was stirring the streets of Madrid. The clouds that had darkened the night were moving eastward.

Francisco looked where the sky had cleared. "The stars are very bright in the northwest," he said quietly. "There is considerable light from Asturias."

He turned back to his studio to rekindle the flame. He had work to do.

The End.

Dear Reader,

If, like Gaspar Jovellanos, you appreciate the work of Spanish artists, you may be interested in the following artworks mentioned either as works in progress or characters and events in the narrative. Unless indicated otherwise, they are oil paintings and are listed in the order they appear in the story:

Bartolomé Esteban Murillo:

Beggar Boy (The Flea Picker). 1650. Musee du Louvre, Paris.

Return of the Prodigal Son. 1667–1670. National Gallery of Art, Washington D.C.

St. Elizabeth of Hungary Nursing the Sick. 1672. Church of the Hospital de la Caridad, Seville

The Liberation of Saint Peter. 1667. The State Hermitage Museum, St. Petersburg, Russia.

Francisco de Goya:

Los Caprichos. 1799. Etchings, Plate 2: "They say yes and give their hand;" Plate 14: "What a Sacrifice!" Metropolitan Museum of Art, New York.

Playing at Giants. 1791. Prado Museum, Madrid.

The Pottery Vendor. 1779. Prado Museum, Madrid.

Los Caprichos. Etching, Plate 24: "Is there no remedy?" Metropolitan Museum of Art, New York.

164   The Light in the Painter's Brush

Francisco de Cabarrús. 1788. Banco de Espana, Madrid.

The Duchess of Alba. 1795. Fundacion Casa de Alba, Madrid.

Diego Velázquez

The Waterseller of Seville. 1620. Wellington Museum, Apsley House, London.

Franciso De Goya

The Family of the Duke and Duchess of Osuna. 1788. Prado Museum, Madrid.

Goya in His Studio. 1790–95. Real Academia de Bellas Artes de San Fernando, Madrid.

Josefa Bayeu (?). 1814. Prado Museum, Madrid.

Diego Velázquez

Las Meninas. 1656. Prado Museum, Madrid.

Francisco de Goya

Copy of *Las Meninas*. 1778. Etching, National Library of Spain, Madrid.

The Taurmaquia (Bullfight scenes). 1816. Metropolitan Museum of Art, New York.

Carlos III. 1786. Prado Museum, Madrid.

Giovanni Battista Tiepolo

Allegory of the Grandeur of the Spanish Monarchy. 1764. Fresco, Royal Palace, Madrid.

Francisco de Goya

The Family of Charles IV. 1800. Prado Museum, Madrid.

Don Manuel Godoy. 1801. Real Academia de Bellas Artes de San Fernando, Madrid.

Maja Desnuda. 1797–1800. Prado Museum, Madrid.

Maja Vestida. 1800–1805. Prado Museum, Madrid.

Gaspar Melchor de Jovellanos. 1798. Prado Museum, Madrid.

Disasters of War (85 prints). 1810–1820. Metropolitan Museum of Art, New York.

The Second of May, 1808. 1814. Prado Museum, Madrid.

The Third of May, 1808. 1814. Prado Museum, Madrid.

Los Caprichos, Etching, Plate 43: "The sleep of reason produces monsters." Metropolitan Museum of Art, New York.

Check out Gaspar Jovellanos, Francisco de Goya, Murillo, and Velázquez on the web, or ask your school media specialist to help you locate copies of the artwork. The following may be of interest to you:

Baticle, Jeannine. *Goya Painter of Terrible Splendor.* New York: Harry N. Abrams, Inc. 1994. This small book contains color prints of most of the Goya paintings mentioned in the story, as well as Tiepolo's work.

Tinterow, G. and Lacambre, G. *Manet/Velázquez, the French Taste for Spanish Painting.* New York: The Metropolitan Museum of Art, 2003. This volume contains prints of paintings by Velázquez and Murillo, as well as Goya.

Muhlberger, Richard. *What Makes a Goya a Goya?* New York: The Metropolitan Museum of Art, Viking, 1994. This slim book has many prints of paintings from the story.

Waldron, Ann. *Francisco Goya.* New York: Harry N. Abrams, Inc., 1992. This book has very good color prints of Goya's works.

A Pronunciation Guide
for the names and places in the story of
Francisco de Goya (1746-1828) and
Gaspar Jovellanos (1744-1811).

People

Gaspar Melchor Baltasar de Jovellanos
.... (Gahs-pahr Mehl-chor day Ho-bay-yah-noss)

Francisco José de Goya y Lucientes
.... (Frahn-thees-ko day Goy-ah)

Francisco de Paula Jovellanos
.....................................(Frahn-thees-ko day Pah-oo-lah)

Juan Agustín Ceán Bermúdez
.... (Wahn Thay-ahn Behr-moo-deth)

Martín Zapater.......................(Mahr-teen Thah-pah-tehr)

Benita Jovellanos, Countess of Peñalva
.... (Beh-nee-tah, Peh-nyahl-vah)

Juan Arias de Saavedra
............................(Wahn Ah-ree-ahth day Sah-bay-drah)

Ramon Bayeu.................................(Rah-mohn Bah-yuh)

José Luzán...(Ho-say Loo-thahn)

Michelangelo................................. (Mee-keh-lahn-jay-lo)

Raffaello...(Rah-fah-eh-lo)

Colon...(Ko-lohn)

Pablo de Olavide..............(Pah-blo day Oh-lah-bee-day)

Bartolomé Esteban Murillo
.... (Bar-toe-lo-may Eh-stay-bahn Moo-ree-yo)

Cervantes................... (Ther-bahn-tehs or Ser-bahn-tehs)

Don Quixote...................................... (Dawn Key-ho-tay)

Rocinante ....(Raw-thee-nahn-tay)

Campomanes..................................(Kahm-po-mah-nayth)

Francisco Cabarrús............(Frahn-thees-ko Kah-bah-roo)

La Duquesa de Alba....................(Doo-kay-sah dahl-bah)

La Duquesa de Osuna ....(Doo-kay-sah day Oh-soo-nah)

Diego Velázquez .... (Dee-eh-go Beh-lath-keth)

Josefa Goya.. (Hoe-seh-fah)

Giovanni Battista Tiepolo
.... (Joe-vah-nee Bah-tee-stah Tee-eh-po-lo)

Emmanuel Godoy ....(Eh-mahn-you-ell Go-doy)

Juan Antonio Meléndez Valdés
.... (Wan Ahn-toh-nee-oh Meh-lehn-deth Bahl-deth)

Alejandro... (Ah-lay-hahn-dro)

Echevarria .... (Eh-chay-vah-ree-ah)

Javier..(Hah-bee-air)

Robles ....(Roe-blays or Roe-blayth)

Suarez...(Swahr-eth)

Places

Alcalá de Henares .... (Ahl-cah-lah day Enn-ah-rayth)

Andalusia ....(Ahn-dah-loo-thee-ah)

Asturias..(A-stoor-ee-ahs)

Avila.. (Ah-bee-lah)

Barcelona ....(Bar-thay-lo-nah)

Castile ....(Kah-steel)

Gijón .... (Hee-hohn)

Jadraque ....(Hah-drah-kay)

Jerez de la Frontera......(Heh-reth day lah frohn-tair-ah)

La Mancha ....(Lah Mahn-chah)

Majorca .... (Mah-yore-kah)

Salamanca ....(Sah-lah-mahn-kah)

Seville .... (Say-bee-yeh)

Zaragoza...(Thah-rah-go-thah)

Author's Note

The world of Francisco De Goya and Gaspar Jovellanos teems with diverse characters, real people who interact with them, from Ceán Bermúdez, Martín Olavide, and Saavedra to Charles IV, a Carthusian apothecary, and an Institute librarian. Other characters, namely Elena, her father, and Echevarria, reflect themes expressed in Jovellano's writings and in Goya's *Caprichos* drawings. I added Pedro and Felipe to the story, and since Gaspar wrote often in his *Diarios*, of traveling *a caballo* and loved the trees of his native Asturias, I provided a really fine horse for him named Robles.